GAIL RIC

KU-060-429

BEYOND HER DREAMS

Complete and Unabridged

LINFORD
Leicester

First published in Great Britain in 2020

First Linford Edition
published 2021

A catalogue record for this book is available
from the British Library.

ISBN 978–1–4448–4738–3

Published by
Ulverscroft Limited
Anstey, Leicestershire

Printed and bound in Great Britain by
TJ Books Ltd., Padstow, Cornwall

This book is printed on acid-free paper

BEYOND HER DREAMS

England, 1848. Housemaid Alice is taken from the big house she works in to be the only servant to Mrs Younger. The first person she meets is Daniel, whose friendly face she remembers in the dark, lonely days that follow. She dreams of romance but Daniel has a sweetheart — hasn't he? Then Mrs Younger disappears and it's up to Alice to find her. Will Daniel help or is he too interested in someone else?

New Beginnings

'Miss? Wake up, miss.'

Alice hadn't noticed the carriage coming to a stop. The first thing she saw when she opened her eyes was an attractive male face with a pair of clear hazel eyes looking at her.

She felt groggy with sleep. How many hours had it been since Mrs Fleming shook her awake before daylight and told her to pack her trunk? The mistress was setting up a new household, Mrs Fleming, the housekeeper, told her. She seemed to feel Alice should be proud she'd been chosen to go with her.

Then Alice's heart had stopped as she was pushed up into a carriage. She'd never been in a carriage before.

It was too early for Charlie to be out in the gardens but she looked for him as the carriage flew out of the gate.

Where were they going? She had no way to let the others know she hadn't wanted to go. What was Charlie going to say?

But now, she supposed as she tried to focus on the voice urging her to wake up, they were there and at least there was a friendly face to greet her.

This boy didn't have Charlie's dark good looks but she saw he was taller and broader than Charlie. He helped her out of the carriage and he and the coachman unloaded the trunks and carried them in. Charlie knew he was handsome but this young man had a naturalness about him that Alice, in her sleepy state, liked.

Then the coachman left and Alice stood for a moment, watching. It was like seeing the last connection with her old life disappear. She'd thought the next time she moved it would be to settle into a home of her own with someone she loved. Charlie had even talked about it.

'I'll be head gardener some day,' he'd told her. 'They'll give me my own cottage. Then we can be together.'

It was what she wanted — a life with someone with prospects, putting down roots.

'I could take in sewing to help with the expenses,' she'd said, 'and learn to read.'

'No need, Alice,' Charlie said. 'I'll take care of everything.' He'd bent to kiss her and his hands were tight on her arms. Alice remembered thinking it was all going too fast. 'You're my girl now.'

'Alice, stop daydreaming.' Mrs Fleming bustled out of the new house. 'That's the last of it,' she told the young man with the hazel eyes. 'Thank you, Daniel.' She slipped something into his hand.

Alice bent to begin to drag her small trunk into the house.

'I'll take the last one in,' the man called Daniel said as Mrs Fleming disappeared inside.

Alice hesitated before following him. She shouldn't be using the front entrance but the gardens around the sides of the house were overgrown. The trees and shrubs had been allowed to spread far too close to the house and the grass was waist high on one side. Alice hoped that wasn't the side where the kitchen was.

She'd never be able to open the back door.

She made her way up to the main door. It would be a waste of time trying to find the back entrance and Mrs Fleming would get impatient waiting for her.

Charlie would be awake now and at work. Would the news that she had gone have reached him from inside or was he still looking forward to seeing her later? He got so cross sometimes when she didn't manage to get away.

He couldn't blame her for this, though.

Alice stood in the doorway, uncertain.

There was no sign of the mistress or Mrs Fleming. There was only the young man, Daniel, coming down the stairs.

'Are you the footman?' she asked him. He didn't look like a footman but he was too young to be the butler and too old to be a boot boy. Or perhaps he was the gardener, destined to remind her every day of Charlie.

He laughed. It was a pleasant sound and she thought probably he laughed often. He was agreeable altogether.

More than agreeable. Alice thought she must be half asleep still if she could be so disloyal to Charlie so soon.

'No. I just happened to be passing by. Your Mrs Fleming isn't someone you can say no to, is she?' He smiled as he left. 'I've taken your trunk up to the top. We'll meet again, I'm sure.'

Alice didn't know how or where and he was gone before she could open her mouth to say, 'I hope so'.

She made her way into the house and through to the scullery at the back.

The house felt empty. There was no sign of any friendly kitchen staff already in place. She wondered when they would all arrive because the person bustling down from the kitchen could only be Mrs Fleming.

'This is not as bad as I feared,' she said. 'Make it spotless, Alice, then see what there is for luncheon.'

'Yes, Mrs Fleming.'

The housekeeper left and Alice looked around for the tap and the copper. At least she had a roof over her head and a meal to look forward to. And perhaps the prospect of a friend in the locality. She felt warm inside at the thought of Daniel and his parting smile.

★ ★ ★

Later, Alice found her trunk in a little room in the attic with a small window that looked out on to open country. How kind of the passer-by to bring her trunk up here and to make sure she knew where to find it. If she could snatch a moment alone in daylight hours, Alice thought she would like standing at her window, watching this world. The open land and sky gave her a feeling that wasn't quite happiness and wasn't quite pain, like a yearning for something — but she didn't know what.

★ ★ ★

Alice got down to the kitchen early the first morning and opened the back door to let the air in. It was a struggle to push the door open but she managed to flatten the vegetation enough.

She was preparing breakfast for the mistress and the housekeeper. Mrs Younger, her mistress, might not even want any, she had been so dispirited yesterday. But Alice was hungry. She hoped Mrs Fleming would sit down with her and she could ask where they were and how long they would be staying.

The air coming in was sweet and gradually filled with birdsong. There was always such a clatter going on in the big house they'd come from, Alice had never heard it so clearly. One bird seemed to be calling louder than the others, or was closer to the house.

As she rechecked the cupboards for something to tempt the mistress, an older man appeared at the open door.

'Good morning,' he called softly, as though not to startle her. 'I've brought your delivery,' he said.

'Oh.' Mrs Fleming hadn't said anything about that.

'Ah, Mr Hopkin.' The housekeeper

bustled in. 'Unpack the order, Alice.'

So that was where Mrs Fleming had hurried off to the afternoon before, leaving Alice cleaning. She had to be grateful the housekeeper was a good organiser, even if she was endlessly telling Alice what to do.

Alice had been in service for more than five years now and worked her way up from lowly scullery maid. She knew what needed doing without being told every minute.

The kind-looking man helped her put the goods on the big table. Apples, mushrooms, potatoes; a loaf of bread and a jar of jam. And herbs. The rich scent caught in Alice's throat and made her heart ache as she remembered the gardens at the house she'd come from.

The cook, who knew the names of all of them, sometimes sent her out to pick some herbs and they'd release their aroma as soon as you touched them. Sometimes she would sit with another of the maids for five minutes in the sun beside where they grew and the stone would be hot to the touch.

They would talk about what was going on in the house and sometimes about their hopes for the future.

Mrs Fleming bustled the delivery man away, checked on the progress of breakfast and hurried off again before Alice could get a word in to ask when the other staff were arriving. Perhaps there weren't any.

A couple of days later, still with no other staff, the same man appeared with a new lot of produce.

'Good morning, Mr Hopkin.' Alice held out her arms for the goods as the song of the bird she'd been listening to got louder. 'Do you know what bird that is?'

He smiled.

'That's a robin. They're often the first ones to wake up and make their claim to their territory.'

'Are they big birds? It seems very loud.'

'No, they're quite small — they're the little brown ones with the red feathers at their throat. That one's looking for a wife and she's listening out for the one who sings best.'

Alice laughed. Then it almost seemed as though the robin stopped singing when he heard Mrs Fleming come in, scolding.

'Come on, Alice, get those eggs put away. We haven't got all day. You haven't even swept the stairs yet.'

Alice thought Mr Hopkin looked uncomfortable as he left but he didn't catch her eye. He was shy, perhaps. She would like to talk to him some more, though, and he didn't seem unwilling to engage with her.

Once Mrs Fleming had bustled out and then back in again to give Alice a list of tasks to do, Alice stepped out of the back door. Mr Hopkin had beaten a trail through the overgrown garden and she could see where the path had once been. She stooped to pull up a handful of tall grass and weeds to see if she could clear the path herself.

A hundred small creatures scurried in all directions, suddenly deprived of their cover. After a few more handfuls she stopped. She trod with difficulty to the end and back. It was going to take longer than a day to make her path.

There was rustling in the nearby bushes.

'Hello, there,' Alice said softly. 'Are you my robin?' She couldn't see through the branches what creature was there. 'Did you find your wife? I wonder if I'll ever know. I hope you will look after her well.' Alice peered for a moment longer. 'And she you.'

On Sunday afternoon they walked to the church, Alice trailing behind Mrs Younger and Mrs Fleming as befitted her place. She had thought their house was isolated but on leaving by the front door it was a short walk to what seemed to be the main street and there were several cottages in a row a few dozen steps away, small, but with neat little gardens bounded by walls.

She kept getting left behind because her eyes were everywhere, first looking back to see if their house formed part of a larger estate and then looking at the countryside, the houses and the people

11

approaching the church. Every now and then she found she had to scurry to catch the other two women up.

They all hesitated for a long time once inside. Alice guessed her mistress was waiting for the sexton to show them to a vacant pew but he ignored them. Alice didn't think anyone would treat the gentry so rudely. It was shocking.

Eventually a kind lady in black made space for two and Alice escaped thankfully to the back where she made herself as small as possible among the other servants.

There was a certain amount of elbow nudging and Alice had the uncomfortable feeling the maids were talking about her. The most talkative seemed to be a girl at the end of the pew with blonde hair streaming to her shoulders. She looked free and relaxed, the opposite of the way Alice felt.

Alice tried to look unconcerned but knew her face was stiff. She didn't know whether the attention was because she was new or because her mistress had been slighted. Alice couldn't wait for the service to be over and she would be able to escape.

Then, unexpectedly, someone from a few pews in front of hers turned around, caught her eye and nodded to her, with a broad smile. So Daniel was here!

And wasn't that Mr Hopkin in the same pew, together with a woman and children of various sizes? It must be Daniel's family. Alice had a sudden wish that she could sit with them away from the unfriendly back pew.

The girls beside her noticed the look from Daniel as well and after some urgent discussion and place changing suddenly the blonde girl was beside her.

'I'm Ivy,' the girl whispered, looking at Alice.

'Alice.'

'I work for Miss Little — she's the lady your mistress is sitting with,' Ivy went on. 'Maybe they'll be friends and we can be friends as well.'

Alice tried to smile. She felt rather afraid of the confident Ivy.

'Do you live there, too?'

Ivy stifled a snort of laughter.

'I do what I think needs doing,' she said. 'My family lives in the village and I live with them. This morning I slept so long I missed the morning service.' She laughed again. 'What about you?'

'Me?' Alice didn't quite understand the question. 'I haven't got any family. I've been with this mistress since my aunt died.' She hesitated. 'I don't even know where we are.'

People were starting to turn round and shush them. Oh, dear. Alice hoped she hadn't brought more attention to her mistress.

The service was coming to an end anyway. She half hoped Mrs Younger would stay behind and talk to the rector so she could chat with Ivy — or better still, talk to Daniel again — but the mistress and Mrs Fleming hurried away with their heads down and Alice had no choice but to follow them. She looked back but couldn't see Daniel or Mr Hopkin.

Alice wondered if one day she would

be proper friends with the outgoing Ivy and would stay to chat after the service.

More than that, she couldn't get that friendly smile and those twinkling hazel eyes out of her mind, or the idea of getting to know the pleasant Hopkin family.

Making Friends

Alice began to look forward to deliveries arriving. The nice farmer was not very talkative but he readily answered her and she had no other human contact apart from Mrs Fleming scolding her.

'What's that bird?' she asked Mr Hopkin one morning. 'It's not the robin.'

'Ah, that's the blackbird. That's your shiny black one with the yellow beak.'

You had to listen hard but that was two she could pick out when they were all up and singing together. She hoped they would all find the right one to pair up with.

She wondered if Charlie would look for someone else or if he was still hoping she'd come back. She imagined him as a self-assured male bird singing loudest to attract his mate.

Now Alice thought she hadn't exactly answered his call but that he'd pursued her just because she hadn't. One of the parlour maids found excuses every day to talk to him and liked to hint that Charlie liked her best. Alice's friend Betty said she thought it was just trouble making.

She hoped Betty was all right and not missing her. Would somebody have explained to them all where Alice had gone or would they be thinking she had chosen to go off and leave them without a word?

Here in the quiet house she began to admit it felt like a burden lifted to know Charlie wasn't outside and wouldn't be making demands of her. She'd allowed her wish for a home of her own and to imagine Charlie would provide it. This far away, she could imagine that Charlie had been looking for something different. There had to be a reason to pursue the one female bird that didn't respond to your plumage and your call.

One afternoon, Mrs Fleming came in with a pile of clothes.

'I've found somewhere to send our laundry, Alice. The laundress, Violet, will come to collect it tomorrow. This is ready to go, if you could just check it

17

over for any mending that needs to be done.' She looked at Alice doubtfully. 'You didn't do any sewing in the other house, did you?'

'I can sew, Mrs Fleming.' Oh dear, perhaps she shouldn't have said that. If she'd said 'no' Mrs Fleming might have got the laundress to do it, or done it herself. Why did she always distrust that people would see her value and have to try to prove they were right to employ her?

Mrs Fleming looked pleased, though. That would have to be enough. It meant a late night stitching and then an early morning taking the sheets off the beds to be ready for the laundress to collect early in the morning.

The laundress turned out to be a tall, broad woman with strong-looking arms, who took the parcel of laundry Alice struggled to lift as if it were nothing.

Alice was grateful not to have to do the laundry herself, but exchanging a few polite words would have been welcome, though Violet looked slightly intimidating. She was in such a hurry, too.

At least Alice had the next Sunday to look forward to. However, Sunday progressed without any sign of preparations to go out.

'May I go to church to the evening service?' Alice asked Mrs Fleming.

'Not today.'

So all she had to look forward to was another lonely week sweeping floors and peeling vegetables.

One day the delivery didn't arrive and Mrs Fleming was put out because her planned menu would have to change. It was just as well the mistress was eating so little these days and sometimes it appeared to Alice that the food came back untouched.

Alice was preparing vegetables. The constant scrubbing had made her knuckles red raw and they hurt. There was a sound at the back door but instead of Mr Hopkin, a plump woman stood there smiling. It was the woman she had seen in church with Mr Hopkin. This must be Daniel's mother. Alice dashed away her tears and reached out to relieve the woman of the baskets.

'You're crying.' The woman put her load on the table and turned to face Alice, kindness and concern on the open freckled face. Alice found herself in a warm pair of arms sobbing against a dress that smelled of apples.

She'd never wept in anyone's arms before. Perhaps in her mother's but she would have been very small and remembered nothing of those times. Never in her aunt's. Her aunt hadn't been unkind to her and her last thought before she died was to make sure the fourteen-year-old Alice had a good place to go to with the Youngers, which Alice was grateful for. But she had never been motherly like this woman.

Except that being comforted while you cried seemed to make it worse, not better.

'Mrs Hopkin!' Mrs Fleming seemed to have an uncanny ability to know if there was anyone else in the scullery. 'What are you doing here?'

'I've brought the delivery, miss.' She

20

still had her arms around Alice. 'My husband is ill. And so, it seems, is your kitchen maid.'

'Alice is not ill. She's feeling sorry for herself and needs to get on with paring the potatoes for Mrs Younger's dinner.'

Alice felt as though the woman was reluctant to let her go but she turned towards the door.

'Can Alice come to church with us on Sunday? I noticed she wasn't there last week.' She looked at Alice. 'Or do you have prayers here?' she asked gently.

Alice knew that if she opened her mouth she would hiccup with the aftermath of the bout of crying. She shook her head and noticed Mrs Fleming looking uncomfortable.

'She can walk with us,' Mrs Hopkin said as if the matter was settled. 'We'll come and collect her for the evening service and bring her back.'

So later in the day, her hands still hurt, and so did her knees, but Alice was humming to herself in the scullery. At last she had something to look forward to, other than learning to identify birds by their tunes and the satisfaction of keeping the household running.

If she kept her head down she might even get a bonus on payday. She had nothing to spend her money on but some savings would bring security. Maybe eventually she would be able to start a little sewing business. She'd missed out on any other education but her aunt had at least taught her to sew well.

There was a knock at the back door and she hoped it wouldn't be someone trying to sell them something or asking for alms. Cook at the big house was for ever having to send strangers away. Alice had sometimes seen her slip some bread or a tasty morsel into their hands before they turned to go.

This was a different sort of place, though. Suppose everyone found out and she let herself in for an endless stream of beggars? It was so difficult to know what to do.

She opened the door.

'Daniel!' This was not expected.

'Ma sent me with some salve for your poor hands,' he said. 'She says to rub it well in and to keep it on for as long as you can without getting them wet.'

'That is kind.'

'Pa didn't think you'd be allowed to sit for long with the potion on but Ma said just a moment will be better than nothing.' He handed the jar over, looking with sympathy at Alice's red hands. So the taciturn farmer had missed nothing.

'I could see if I could keep some of it on while I'm polishing the silver.'

Daniel put his hand into his pocket.

'There's something else.'

Alice turned to put the jar on the table inside and he followed her in, drawing out a bundle of leaves.

He gestured to her hands. This close, Charlie had always smelled of some potion he put on his hair, even for the work day. Daniel smelled of the sweet fresh fields he must have been walking through and Alice's heart seemed to expand.

'Ma said I have to show you how to do

it. Do you mind, Alice?'

She offered him her hands, palms down, and he took the one with the worst cuts in his own hands. They were red and callused but warm and surprisingly gentle. Alice held on to the scullery table with her other hand, suddenly dizzy.

'You draw the edges of the cut together. Tell me if I'm hurting you, Alice.'

She shook her head. His hands were full of cuts of their own that looked as though they had healed over before another one appeared close to it. But for all their hardness from years of toil his touch was so tender it took her breath away.

'Then cover it with one of the leaves.' He placed one gently on her knuckle. 'It knits the skin together again.'

When it was done he didn't relinquish her hand and there was no sound except the beating of Alice's heart filling her ears.

He heard Mrs Fleming coming before she did. He laid her hand beside the other one on the edge of the table and stepped towards the door.

'Good afternoon, Mrs Fleming.'

It felt cold when he moved away.

'What are you doing here? We had the delivery earlier.'

Alice opened her mouth to explain Mrs Hopkin's kindness but stopped before she spoke because Mrs Fleming would have no sympathy and might send the potion away with Daniel.

'My ma sent me to ask if you would like me to tidy your side alley,' he said easily. 'It doesn't bother Pa but she said it's a job for anyone else to get down it.' He didn't look at Alice. 'I've got my tools outside.'

Mrs Fleming herself would be unaware of the difficulties, Alice reflected. She'd become cook as well as housekeeper since they'd been here just as Alice had become scullery maid, housemaid and everything in between. On the other hand Mrs Fleming had also become lady's maid and companion to Mrs Younger and would never think to use the back entrance.

'Well.' Mrs Fleming stood and thought.

'That might be a good idea. We don't want to be missed when the knife grinder comes round.' She nodded. 'Thank you, Daniel, and please thank your mother.'

Daniel grinned and went outside.

Alice felt a stab of something like happiness to know Daniel was here and the Hopkins were looking out for her.

* * *

Alice's thoughts confused her in bed that night. She hadn't always liked Charlie kissing and touching her. So how could it be that when Daniel, whom she barely knew, was close to her, she'd longed for him to put his arms around her and hold her?

A visitor came to the front door as Alice was changing into her Sunday best for church. Her first thought was that she might not now be allowed out.

She crept quietly down the stairs, trying to ignore the loud male voice in the front parlour.

'Eleanor, this is most irregular. Where

is John?'

Alice had barely ever seen the master of the big house and had been taught to lower her eyes if their paths crossed but she knew his name was John Younger. Had she known the mistress was Eleanor? There was a recollection of someone called Lady Eleanor but that must be someone else.

'Edward, don't shout at me.'

'As your only brother, I have the duty to maintain what is proper in the family.' Alice could hear the mistress's brother pacing loudly up and down. 'You misled me when you asked to take this property. You led me to understand it was for a week only and John would be here with you.'

'I'm sure I did not intend to mislead.'

'You know I have sold all the land here and only the lodge house remains. It is not close enough to my new estate for me to afford you my protection.'

'I don't need your protection, Edward.'

'Oh, I think you do. You can't stay here with only two servants — female servants at that. It is not seemly and means I can't let my agent stay here when he needs to.' He continued his loud pacing and his voice rose. 'It is most inconvenient, Eleanor. And John doesn't even know where you are.'

'Did John send you to find me?'

Alice thought the mistress's brother wasn't going to answer.

'No,' he said eventually. 'The gossip in the village reached me and I wrote to John.'

'There.' Mrs Younger sounded more energetic now. 'He doesn't want me back, does he?'

So she had left Mr Younger. That was what all this was about. It was true Mrs Younger had never looked very happy in the last few years but she was secure and lived well. Why throw that away?

There was another hesitation.

'Regardless of what either of you want or don't want, I am here to escort you back to your husband.'

Alice fled silently. They wouldn't leave her behind. Without her the packing and clearing up wouldn't be completed. She would have her afternoon out whatever Mrs Younger's brother made them do afterwards.

Alice hurried up the cleared path beside the house and down to the road beyond where Daniel waited with a younger girl almost as tall as him.

'This is my sister, Maggie,' Daniel explained.

'Are you being thrown out?' the girl asked, linking her arm through Alice's. 'That man owns the lodge where you live. And the land our pa farms and our house as well, but we never see him around here.'

'He's the mistress's brother,' Alice said. 'Somebody sent for him to make her to go back to her husband.' As soon as the words were out, Alice put her other hand to her mouth. Two seconds out of the house and she was gossiping about her mistress's private life. However, she soon learned there were no secrets.

'Yes,' the girl said. 'Everyone in the village is scandalised. Any number of

29

them could have sent for him.'

'My money's on the curate.'

'Daniel!' the girl said.

'What, Maggie? I know you favour Miss Little but I'm sure I'm right.'

'I said no such thing. Miss Little would never do anything like that. I might have said someone in . . . Oh, you know exactly what I meant.'

They both laughed as though it wasn't the most shocking thing in the world to be talking so.

'Ma feels sorry for your mistress,' Maggie went on. 'She says it's losing so many babies has made her too sad.'

This was something else for Alice to think about. She'd never heard such personal talk. The mistress had often been ill over the years and the servants were hushed from discussing the cause.

'How do you find these things out?'

'There's nothing you can't find out in this place if you've a mind to,' Maggie said. 'We know you're Alice and you're an orphan and work for the Youngers. We know they're cruel to you and you need us for friends.'

'They're not cruel to me,' Alice said.

'No,' Daniel agreed. 'Pa says only he works longer hours than you but at least he has the land to glory in and no-one looking over his shoulder to tell him he's doing everything wrong.'

Maggie squeezed Alice's arm and they caught up with the rest of the family.

'Come back with us for supper afterwards, Alice,' Mrs Hopkin called.

'I don't think I should,' Alice answered. 'We may be leaving.'

'All the more reason to come.'

Alice hesitated as they got to the entrance to the church but on either side of her Maggie and Daniel continued walking towards the pew they'd been in the week before and she found herself sitting between the brother and sister. Alice glanced round and smiled at Ivy in the back pew. Ivy frowned back.

This was unexpected. Did Alice now have to worry that she might not be able to be friends with Ivy as well as the Hopkin family?

She could feel Daniel's warmth in the pew beside her. It was unfortunate about Ivy but for once Alice was exactly where she wanted to be.

Hopes Dashed

At the end of the service they all spilled out into the churchyard as Alice had witnessed the first week. It warmed her heart to be part of it this time. Mr and Mrs Hopkin began to talk to a group of adults while the younger children found their friends and began a sedate game. Daniel and Maggie started chatting to other young people.

Alice felt uncertain again until Ivy joined her with a smile.

'Too good to sit with us at the back?' she asked.

Did the smile mean it was a joke? There was something in the intonation that made Alice unsure.

'I couldn't be rude to Mrs Hopkin.'

'No, of course not.' Ivy turned abruptly and got hold of Alice's upper arm to guide her. 'Come on. I need to see whether my sweetheart has left me anything.'

Alice glanced over her shoulder nervously.

'I don't want Mrs Hopkin to think I've left without saying anything.'

'Don't be such a mouse, Alice.' She laughed as if to take the sting out of the comment. 'They'll be gossiping for ages. Anyway, it's only round here.'

They picked their way through the gravestones and before long Alice found herself standing in front of one that looked very old. Ivy put her hand behind the worn, crooked headstone and drew it back out again, empty.

'Have you got a young man?' Ivy asked as she started to move away. 'You don't look so bad with your hair down and grey is an unusual colour for eyes.' For a moment Alice didn't know what to say. She didn't know what to make of this changeable girl at all. 'So have you?'

'Yes.' It might not be true any more that she had a young man, if it ever was. But she'd been called a mouse and didn't want to seem so. The story of a follower might make Alice seem more interesting.

Ivy looked surprised and, Alice

thought, not entirely pleased.

'A local boy?' she asked suspiciously.

'No, from the house where I was before. I'm a bit worried because they took me out early in the morning and brought me here so he might not know where I am . . . '

'Is he a footman?'

'No, a gardener.'

'Footmen have better prospects. Is he the head gardener?'

'An under-gardener.'

'What's his name?'

It was almost as though Ivy didn't believe he existed and was trying to catch Alice out.

'Charlie. Once he becomes head gardener he'll get a cottage of his own and we can live there.'

It was like talking about someone else. Had she really agreed to marry him or was she just taken up with the idea of being secure in her own house? He might stop her learning to read and making some money of her own. He did get cross when she opposed him.

'What's your sweetheart's name, Ivy?'

Ivy gave a secret smile.

'I can't tell you. We're not telling anyone yet. He's not able to marry at the moment.'

Alice nodded.

'Is he in service?'

'Mmm, not exactly.'

They rounded the corner of the church and almost collided with Maggie on the path.

'Oh, there you are, Alice.' Maggie nodded at Ivy. 'How are you, Ivy?' When Ivy didn't answer Maggie turned back to Alice. 'We're going now.'

'Goodbye, Ivy.' Alice waited for a few seconds before she went with Maggie but Ivy didn't reply.

It was odd that two such sociable girls in their different ways didn't seem like friends. From her own position, Alice didn't feel she was able to pick and choose and wanted to know both of them better.

Nevertheless, Alice resisted the temptation to go for supper at the Hopkins' this time. She was reliant on the good-will of her employers and it felt wilful to linger when they may need her.

As it happened, the mistress's brother had left by the time Alice got back and Mrs Fleming said nothing about Alice's outing, the visit from the mistress's brother or about them leaving.

As she finished tidying the kitchen that night, Alice regretted not going to the Hopkins' after church. They would hardly have missed her here. When she could pluck up the courage she would ask for Sunday to be her day off.

She imagined going for walks with Ivy and having supper at Maggie's house after church, getting to know both of them better. The whole Hopkin fam-ily, in fact. Including Daniel. Especially Daniel.

Would it be worth making a life for herself here if she could once again be lifted out of it and taken back to where they'd come from? Thinking of Daniel and his smile and his clear gaze, she knew she wanted to try to make a life here. It could be worth it.

It definitely could.

Mrs Fleming got herself ready to go out the next afternoon and Alice wondered if the mistress would go, too, and she'd be left alone, or if they wanted her to accompany them and she'd have another chance to go out. She longed to see more of the surroundings.

'The mistress is having a sleep,' Mrs Fleming told her. 'You must listen in case she rings. She may want tea when she wakes up.'

'Yes, Mrs Fleming.'

Mrs Fleming hesitated for a moment longer, then left. This was different from when she bustled off to arrange a delivery or a service. Alice heard the front door close and once again she'd missed the opportunity to ask questions or see if she could always have Sundays off.

Ivy was right. She was a mouse.

The mistress didn't ring and Alice realised she was spending a lot of time in her room. Was she sleeping? Perhaps she was ill. She wondered if Mrs Hopkin had a remedy for it.

That reminded her. She put some of the salve on her cracked knuckles and sat listening to the creaking of the old house and hoping it was not scuttling sounds she could hear from the kitchen.

Mrs Fleming came back almost cheerful from wherever she'd been and Alice felt as though she'd had a holiday herself, taking her time with her tasks and giving herself a moment to sit in the quiet and heal her broken skin.

She could almost feel something else healing inside her as well as her thoughts quietened and she forgave herself for the wrong choices she had made. She didn't even feel that she had chosen Charlie, more that he had pursued her until she couldn't resist any more. Perhaps it was the pursuit that he liked.

★ ★ ★

'Mrs Fleming?' she asked that night when the housekeeper brought the plates down after her and Mrs Younger's

39

dinner and Alice prepared to wash them. 'Am I all right to go to church again on Sunday?'

Mrs Fleming hesitated.

'We could have prayers here, I suppose. But I don't know if the mistress would want to.'

'I've always been to church.'

Mrs Fleming knew very well there had been occasions when none of the household had gone if John Younger had important guests, but she and the butler at the house Alice had come from had both talked about being responsible for the spiritual welfare of the staff. Mrs Fleming may be strict but she knew her duty.

'Very well. Go to the afternoon service. The mistress may be sleeping then in any case.'

'And if Mrs Hopkin asks me for supper, may I go? I haven't had a day off since we've been here.'

'Well, nor have I, but I suppose you're a good girl and may have Sunday afternoons off, providing Mrs Younger has nothing planned.'

'Thank you, Mrs Fleming.'

That was settled then. Alice was not a mouse at all. She was a housemaid who did her work well and had Sunday afternoons off.

If the invitation to supper wasn't repeated she would be able to walk a little and get to know the area. Or Ivy or one of the other girls might invite her. Or if they didn't, or if it rained, she could slip up to her room and lie on her own bed dreaming.

When he brought the next delivery Mr Hopkin greeted Alice kindly, as he always did. He put the baskets on the table and turned to Alice.

'If your Mrs Fleming is nowhere near,' he began in a low voice, 'do come out to the alley with me. There is something you will like to see.'

Alice nodded, intrigued, and stepped out behind him.

'Tread softly.'

Half way along the alley, in the deepest of the undergrowth and well away from the path, there was a flash of movement.

'We mustn't disturb them or they'll leave and her work will be for nothing.'

Barely breathing, Alice leaned over. She would never have spotted the nest if Mr Hopkin hadn't shown her. It looked prickly on the outside but inside it was as if leaves had been smoothed over. That would be cosy and safe.

'Is it my robin's? Is he building his nest here?'

Mr Hopkin nodded and drew her away, back to the door.

'It'll be his wife doing the building, while he feeds her.'

Alice laughed.

'Of course. But it seems very low down. Will they be safe?'

'It's well hidden. They know what they're doing.'

Alice hoped the little nest-builder had chosen her mate well. Had she picked him because he sang the loudest or was there something else that attracted her? And had he chosen her because he thought she'd work hard or was she beautiful?

'Thank you for showing me,' she told Mr Hopkin and he reflected her own broad smile.

Ivy also had a big smile on her face when she joined Maggie and Alice in the churchyard after the service the next Sunday. Daniel had been with them one minute and vanished the next. Maggie also saw another friend to talk to and left Ivy and Alice alone. So she wasn't wrong that Maggie didn't like Ivy and it looked as though maybe Daniel didn't, either.

Ivy frowned a little in the direction Daniel had gone but she seemed to be bursting with her news.

'Who do you think has visited Miss Little this week? Do you know?'

'Not my mistress's brother?' Alice's heart was in her mouth. If he owned a lot of the land and properties he would visit the neighbours. If this was the lady in black who had let Mrs Younger into her pew on the first Sunday perhaps he would try to turn her against his sister.

'No, silly. He never comes near and

even his agent never stays for tea. But somebody else you know.'

Alice's head became a confusion of thoughts. She only knew the Hopkins and had no knowledge of who they called on.

Ivy came to her rescue.

'Your Mrs Fleming.'

Ah. That explained where the house-keeper had gone.

'I wonder why.'

'She wants advice about what to do with Lady Eleanor, I expect.'

'Who?'

'Your mistress.'

'She's not called that.' As soon as she said it Alice wondered if she was wrong. She remembered her mistress being called Eleanor.

'She is around here. That's what she was called before she married, apparently, when they all lived up at the park behind your lodge.' Ivy linked arms with Alice and began to walk. 'The park isn't there any more, of course. Maybe she was something special then but she seems a dowdy creature these days.'

Alice had never thought about it. There weren't many visitors to the house she'd come from and she'd only occasionally seen Mrs Younger dressed to go out. She was the best-dressed woman Alice had seen. Here she had no reason to put fine clothes on — nobody called and she went nowhere.

'She hasn't brought her jewels and finery with her,' she told Ivy.

'Is that what they told you to say?'

'No.' Alice was confused. 'I clean and put everything away. I'd have seen it.'

'They'll have hidden them,' Ivy said confidently. 'You have a look and tell me if I'm right.'

Alice knew she would do no such thing.

'But what did you mean about needing advice?'

'About her leaving her husband and nobody talking to her. Her staying at home and not bothering with visits isn't making her popular, either.'

'What is she supposed to do if everyone ignores her?'

'Hold her head up high and act like everything's normal.' Ivy tossed her head. 'That's the way to act.'

'Did your mistress tell Mrs Fleming that?'

'I don't know. I couldn't really hear. Except your Mrs Fleming did ask about the boy who comes in to do the heavy work at our place.'

'You have other help?'

'Of course. There's a daily cook as well. Maybe you're going to get other help, too. Or you're going to get sent back and they'll get other staff.'

'Did you hear them say that?'

'No, but it would be nice, wouldn't it, Alice, to go back to your Charlie?' Ivy looked at her closely.

A strange feeling crept over Alice. She knew she should say yes but it wasn't true.

The opposite was true.

'Wouldn't it?' Ivy insisted.

'It would.' She wanted a husband who would be like Mr Hopkin as he got older, caring about strangers and knowing about birdsong. Charlie wasn't that man, she was certain. 'He may have forgotten about me by now.'

Ivy squeezed her arm.

'Why would you say that? You haven't forgotten about him.'

'No.' She blushed as she realised she was interested in someone else now. 'How often does someone come in to help with the heavy work at your place?' She needed to prevent Ivy talking about Charlie, it confused her so.

'Stanley? Not so often now Miss Little sends the laundry out.' Ivy laughed. 'She got tired of me dropping the clean sheets all the time, even with Stanley there to put them through the mangle. But she gets him in to take the curtains down and beat the carpets. She says he does it better than me and it suits me not to have to do those jobs.'

'You don't work there every day?'

'It depends on my family. And other things.'

Alice wondered at what Miss Little put up with. A maid at the big house

47

who didn't beat carpets and didn't even come in if her family needed her would not be in employment for long.

'I expect Stanley could find time to do some work for your Mrs Fleming. We do wonder how you manage, only women.'

'Ivy, Stanley is not your sweetheart, is he?' Ivy seemed to be repeating the name for the joy of hearing it.

Heads in the vicinity turned at the sound of Ivy's laughter.

'Sorry, Alice, you're not to know. But if you were to see him you'd know why I laugh so.'

Ivy disappeared when they started on the road home and saw coming towards them the lady in black who had been at the service that first Sunday. Alice could see why Ivy might not want to meet her employer on her day off but the woman must have seen her and wondered at her rudeness.

'Good evening, Miss Little,' Mrs Hopkin said.

Alice looked with interest. So this was the person who may have informed her mistress's brother, according to Maggie. Was that how the conversation had gone? But she was good to Ivy. And to Mrs Fleming, apparently. She was slim and smiling as she moved her umbrella from hand to hand as she got her gloves on.

'Good evening,' the woman said politely. 'I trust your husband and little one are both better.'

'Completely recovered, thank you,' Mrs Hopkin said. She pointed to the two younger children who were running backwards and forwards and laughing. 'As you see. It was but a two-day cold.'

Miss Little smiled and looked at her hands before one glove fell to the ground. Alice darted forward and picked it up.

'Thank you, my dear. You must be Alice.' She turned to walk in the other direction, the way Alice and the Hopkins were headed. 'Walk with me for a moment, my dear. How are you finding life here?' she asked kindly. 'It must have been hard to leave your friends so suddenly.'

Alice fell into step with her, Daniel and Maggie in front.

'I'm getting used to it here, thank you, miss.'

'And your young man?' Miss Little added. 'Have you heard from him?'

Maggie glanced behind as if she could hear the conversation and Daniel speeded up, holding Maggie's arm to make sure she kept up with him.

How did Miss Little know about that? She'd told no-one but Ivy and surely Ivy wouldn't gossip with her employer.

'No, miss.'

Miss Little nodded, then called her goodbyes to the Hopkins and patted Alice's arm again.

'We'll speak again,' she said and turned round to go home.

Maggie and Daniel waited for her to catch them up and took up their places one each side of Alice.

'She's kind, isn't she, Miss Little?' Daniel said, looking at Alice.

'She does seem so,' Alice said. 'Very kind.'

'You didn't tell us you had a young man,' Maggie said.

'She doesn't have to tell us everything, Maggie.'

'I don't know who could have told Miss Little,' Alice said. 'I haven't spoken of him to anyone.'

'Your housekeeper has visited Miss Little,' Maggie said.

'I know, but she doesn't know about Charlie.' Alice hesitated. 'I didn't think she knew. And why would she talk of it to Miss Little?'

Alice was becoming confused. Her friendship with Charlie was becoming less important to her as time went on and here it was becoming over-important again.

'I'm sorry I didn't tell you.'

'You don't have to tell us,' Daniel said again. 'But I think you must have told Ivy.'

'Did Ivy tell you she had a sweetheart?' Maggie asked.

'Maggie, don't.'

'I won't spread it further. I just want

51

to know. She did, didn't she?'

Alice had got into difficulties telling Ivy about Charlie in order to lift herself in Ivy's estimation.

'She said it was a secret.'

'So she didn't tell you who it was?' Maggie asked, looking at Daniel.

'No.'

'Right. That's enough of that conversation.' Daniel's cheeks were rather red, perhaps from the sun or the exertion of the walk. Or because of something else. Ivy and Daniel. They would make a handsome couple, it was true. Or it was someone else and it affected Daniel that Ivy had a follower.

As the brother and sister continued their conversation about other things, Alice stayed quiet, unable to name the small cold space inside her where a secret hope had died.

Getting To Know You

It was so easy to be with the Hopkin family and they were so solicitous Alice soon recovered her spirits and vowed that her friendship with everyone in this family wouldn't be spoiled over a silly fancy.

'Don't crowd Alice,' Daniel told the younger children as once in the house they clamoured for her attention.

'Have you got brothers and sisters?' one of the boys asked.

'No.'

'Nor parents, either?' The littlest girl put her hand sympathetically on Alice's arm.

'My father died when I was a baby and my mother when I was four,' Alice explained. 'Fortunately, my aunt took me in but she had no children.'

'See how lucky we are,' Mr Hopkin said, looking around. 'Twenty-seven of you all fit and healthy.'

There were peals of laughter.

'Twenty-seven!'

'Or does it only seem so when you're all talking at once? It must give our poor guest quite the headache.'

The little ones were dispatched outside when they had eaten enough and Mr Hopkin soon followed. There were chores to do before dark.

Once only Mrs Hopkin and the two older children were left, the tiny farmhouse kitchen seemed to expand. They were indeed lucky to have one another and Alice now felt her attic room and the big scullery were going to seem even emptier.

'Your aunt died, too, didn't she?' Mrs Hopkin asked, helping Alice to another slice of cold fruit pie.

Alice nodded.

'She found me the place with Mr and Mrs Younger before she passed.'

'Are we to tell our life stories as well, so Alice doesn't feel she's the only one?' Daniel asked, finishing his own pie.

'Alice knows it's only because we care for her welfare,' his mother said easily.

'I do and I thank you kindly for it,'

Alice said. 'But I would love to know something of your lives, too.' She looked at the three, careful not to catch Daniel's eye.

'My husband and I have been farming here since we married. Our plot is getting smaller but we have enough to feed ourselves and pay the rent.'

'We might open a shop one day,' Maggie said.

'But we can't manage it yet,' Mrs Hopkin added. 'Daniel is apprenticed to be a thatcher and it's fortunate that it's with his uncle, my brother, so he allows him some days to come and work on our piece of land here. In return my brother gets his provisions.'

Alice looked at Daniel.

'Does that mean your training will take longer?' She'd heard talk of apprenticeships in the servants' hall where she'd worked before. It seemed long for those concerned but it would be secure to have a trade. A security out of the reach of Alice and the rest of the servants.

'Daniel will work with his uncle when

the training is done so what he doesn't learn in these next years he will pick up after. He's the only one of us who has travelled more than a mile or two away from home, when they have work to do further afield.'

'You do not wish to travel, Ma.' Daniel looked fondly at his mother.

She laughed.

'No. Alice will have seen more of the country than us.'

'Oh.' Alice laughed, too. 'I slept most of the way here.'

'They woke you up early, didn't they?' Daniel said. 'You couldn't have known there would be villagers quizzing you on what you'd seen.'

'We would love you to stay, Alice, but it's starting to get dark. Let Daniel walk you home.'

'There's no need. I think I know the way.' Alice was not sure she did but did not want them to feel they had to take her. 'But let me help wash the pots first.'

'Not today, Alice.' Mrs Hopkin smiled and got up to clear the table. 'I'm sure you will help another time but Maggie will do it today.'

So Maggie wouldn't be coming with them. Alice covered her confusion with her thanks and goodbyes and then she was in the lane and Daniel was beside her, warm and solid and sure of where he was going.

'I hope we weren't too noisy and boisterous for you,' Daniel said as they set off.

'Not at all. Your family has been so generous to me. I'll never be able to repay you all.'

Alice glanced to the side and saw Daniel was looking at her. She stumbled over a hole in the ground and he put a hand out to steady her, then moved closer.

'Take my arm, Alice.'

She did and they walked in silence for a moment. Alice found it difficult to breathe.

'So long as we don't meet your Charlie come to look for you.' Daniel laughed.

'Or Ivy.' As soon as the words were out Alice regretted them. She wasn't supposed to know.

'No,' Daniel agreed. 'Ivy can find reason to spread tittle-tattle where there is none.'

That wasn't quite what Alice meant.

'Is that why Maggie doesn't like her?'

'Does it show that she doesn't? No, that's not the reason.'

Alice waited to be told the real reason, whether she didn't approve of Ivy stealing her brother's heart or thought she was going to break his heart. But then Daniel asked a surprising question.

'Is it possible that Charlie will come here, do you think?'

Why was he thinking about Charlie? Was it because he cared so much about her wellbeing and thought she was sad? Perhaps he was happy with his Ivy despite the secrecy and wanted everyone to be happy.

But then how could she tell him she no longer cared for Charlie, had never truly cared for Charlie, without seeming flighty?

'No.' It was never so important, she

wanted to say. 'Though I only want to make sure he knows I didn't go willingly without telling him. I wouldn't do that.'

Daniel nodded as though he understood. Alice wondered what he thought he understood. It was all so complicated.

When he didn't speak she asked another question that had been on her mind.

'Are you happy with your uncle? The apprenticeship?'

Daniel looked at her curiously.

'It's good to learn a trade.'

'Didn't you want to follow your father into farming?'

'I might have done, but things are starting to change. The landowner isn't leasing us as much land as he used to. There's not enough work for all of us. My uncle was doing well at the time I was of an age to decide which way to go.

'Some of the boys in the village were going to the factories by then. I wanted to avoid that — or at least my parents wanted to avoid any of us having to do that if they could. Once I've finished the apprenticeship I'll earn better to be able to help with the expenses.'

'Yes,' Alice said, after a pause. Could this explain why Daniel was not free to declare his interest in Ivy? He was committed to helping his parents and his younger brothers and sisters?

'That wasn't what you meant, was it, Alice?' he said then. 'You wanted to know if I'm happy.' He turned to look at her with the same tenderness she had felt when he had put the leaves on her cuts. 'Such a difficult situation you're in and you care about other people's happiness.'

'It's just that your father talks about loving the land. I wondered . . . '

'You saw that I do, too,' he said, nodding. 'But I'm out in the open and from the rooftops I can see further than he does and hear the birds more clearly.'

Alice smiled.

'You've talked to him about our birds.'

'He was impressed that you were so interested, and so caring of the creatures. As for us, he worries. It was never the intention that I would do anything

60

but work the land like him nor Maggie help in the dairy and so on.'

'You didn't yearn to do something different?'

He paused before he answered.

'Never. Does that make me uninteresting to you?'

Alice's heart was calling out to her that she had never been so interested in anyone before but her head advised against saying so and she ended up not replying.

'And your Charlie?' Daniel went on. 'Does he love his gardens?'

Alice hesitated again. Charlie didn't love the plants he tended, she was certain. What did Charlie care for? He had worked in London, she knew, and had a fondness for music halls and, she thought, drinking places. He had talked of dancing. She hadn't asked, hadn't dared to, if it was London he wanted to return to. Could he be a head gardener in a big house in London?

He never talked about his family. She didn't even know where they were or if he had any. Alice had assumed he would tell her everything eventually. Here, after some time away from his commanding presence, that didn't make sense. They didn't have proper conversations, didn't know one another at all.

Now what she really wanted was to shout out loud, 'He's not my Charlie.' He never had been and nor did she want him to be.

'I'm sorry, Alice,' Daniel went on as the silence continued. 'I didn't mean to remind you again.'

'No, no, it's not that, Daniel. I don't think of Charlie any more.' She willed him to understand.

'I like to work on the roofs,' Daniel said after a while, perhaps anxious he hadn't reassured her enough, or perhaps to distract her from thoughts of where she had lived before. 'There is a satisfaction to seeing the new thatch build up and knowing it will keep out the rain and snow and keep a family snug inside.'

Alice smiled.

'And on your days at home to watch

the crops growing to feed them as well.'

Daniel laughed.

'My life is perfect.' He touched her arm. 'Almost perfect.'

Would Ivy complete Daniel's life?

Alice blushed to think how short a time ago it was that she was thinking of being in a cottage with a head gardener coming home to her in the evenings and now her thoughts were of something very different.

And then they were at the house and Daniel was commenting about the vegetation in the side passage growing again and then she was through the door and he'd gone and she was left feeling that nothing was clear between them.

Or that everything was.

'Wake up, miss,' he'd said on that first day. Alice felt her eyes were open at last.

* * *

'Hello, there.' A soft male voice called through the open door. Alice was half expecting the laundry back but this was a man she had never seen before. She hurried to the door and saw he did indeed have the parcel of clothes and linens she'd sent off to be laundered.

He was probably only around Alice's age, from his face, but he was a giant. Very tall and broad with enormous hands that made Alice think he could crush her between his thumb and forefinger and not notice. But he stood away from the doorway not to crowd her and his voice was gentle.

'Good morning, miss. My mother, the laundress, asked me to deliver this back to you.' He offered it to her from a distance. It was as though he had learned to be particularly gentle because of his appearance and ensure strangers knew he wasn't to be feared.

'Thank you.' She reached out for the heavy package. 'I hope your mother is not ailing?'

'Thank you for asking, miss. Let me bring this in for you.' The young man took the laundry into the scullery as Alice stood aside for him. He placed it on the table and immediately returned to the doorway. He smelled of starch and steam.

What a polite young man. Alice found herself wondering about his father because he hadn't learned these manners from his brusque mother.

'My mother is not ailing but behind with the work,' he explained.

'You help her?' She imagined those thick arms would make light work of lifting heavy wet linen to feed through the mangle and hanging it up, still damp, to dry.

He nodded.

'In all but the mending, and it is the mending that holds her up.'

'Our washing will have added to her workload.'

'But my mother said yours was beautifully repaired.' He smiled. 'Was that your work?'

'It was.' Alice wished she had known it could have been done for them.

'She said if the person who did that ever wants to leave her position and come to work with us there would be a place for her.' He was still smiling and there was a beauty to his oversized features and a twinkle in his eyes.

What would it be like working in a laundry? Alice remembered the constant damp in the air and the hiss of steam, and the laundry maids' hands being more red and sore than her own, sometimes up to the elbows, what with the heat of the water and the yellow soap and stain removers they used.

No wonder the laundress, who did loads for more than one household, had not much cheery conversation.

She smiled back at the young man, reluctant to tell him how little the prospect appealed, even if it were serious.

'Thank your mother for her kind words.'

He turned to leave.

'Pleased to meet you, miss.'

'I'm Alice.'

He nodded again.

'I'm Stanley.'

Alice watched as he made his way

surprisingly delicately up the side path and disappeared.

So that was Ivy's Stanley? If so, how cruel to laugh at him, as if looks were the only important thing. As if he wasn't a good-looking young man in his own way.

Alice wondered how she could bring the subject up with Ivy, but it was Mrs Hopkin who approached her after church the next Sunday.

'Alice, may I speak to you?'

This was surprising.

'But of course, Mrs Hopkin.'

Alice was conscious that she should not be dawdling this morning because Mrs Fleming was ill.

The housekeeper had greeted her early in the kitchen when looking for a drink for a sore throat and to cool her fever and Alice had hurried her back to bed. She was no trouble to look after but was no better by the time Alice was ready to leave for church. She was not going to forgo her outing but promised to come back after the service. She couldn't see the mistress looking after her sick housekeeper.

'I wanted to speak to you about being in service in a big household. Maggie is due to go up to the big house at Easter.'

'Is she? I didn't know that.'

'We tried to avoid it but our land has been reduced and there is not enough work to keep all the children at home. I'm sorry, Alice, ours may seem a minor problem to you. And Daniel asked me to be careful not to upset you if you are missing your Charlie. I wouldn't ask except that I am beginning to worry about Maggie.'

'Daniel says that? It's not true at all. He must have misunderstood. Charlie was never right for me and I don't think he loved me.'

'Oh.'

'But I had no idea about Maggie,' Alice went on. 'Is it to my mistress's brother's house?'

'Yes. You have never been there but it must be similar to Mr Younger's place.

Or possibly bigger, I don't know. What will it be like for her, Alice? You were the same age as she is now when you started, weren't you?'

'I was just fourteen but I was so different from Maggie,' Alice said. 'I lived a sheltered life with my aunt. There were no other relations and her friends were older and either were childless or their children were grown. I was not used to society and when there was company I was not encouraged to speak.'

'So you found it hard to be with so many other people in the big house?'

'I felt slow and stupid beside the other maids. They seemed like butterflies and I the solid bumblebee at the end of the day, too full of nectar to rise high or speed anywhere.'

'You got used to it?'

'Oh, yes, I grew to like the companionship and getting to know a little of the other people's lives. But it will be different for Maggie. She is quick and clever and is used to gossip and company and

69

already has friends of her own. She will fit in more readily than I did.'

'And the work?'

'It is true the work is hard and the hours long but Maggie is a hard worker here, isn't she? She should not have problems.'

'Maggie is a dreamer, Alice. She gets distracted and ruins the cheese or jam and we can't afford it.'

Alice could see why her family would worry.

'Do you want me to speak to her? Make sure she understands that it is not like here, that she will have to obey the rules?'

'Yes, do speak to her, Alice, before she goes.'

'How long do we have?'

'But a week, now. Until the week before Easter.'

Alice nodded.

'I need to make her understand there will be little time for reading or day-dreaming.'

'Thank you, Alice,' Mrs Hopkin said.

She smiled. 'I feel better since knowing you because you're a dreamer, too, and they haven't made you lose that.'

Danger

The woman Ivy worked for, Miss Little, was making her way to the gate and nodded to Mrs Hopkin and Alice.

'I've been thinking about you and your young man, Alice,' Miss Little said kindly once Mrs Hopkin had rejoined her family. 'You could . . . write to him, perhaps?'

'No. I can't . . . '

'If you wanted help, I'm happy to assist, you know. People in this village gossip so you may have been told this already.' She gave a little laugh. 'When I was around your age I was going to marry and my sweetheart was sent to India. We wrote as often as we could. It was such a comfort I like to offer other young people in the same situation whatever assistance I can.' She glanced again at Alice. 'With stamps, or getting the words down and reading back the replies.'

'That is very kind of you, miss.'

Miss Little lowered her voice.

'And with it would come a promise to never divulge your secrets, of course. If you think you can trust me.'

'What happened to your sweetheart? If you don't mind me asking.'

Miss Little nodded.

'He died in India.'

Alice had feared as much.

'And you've never stopped loving him.'

She felt as though she might never be able to truly tell this woman what her feelings were about Charlie. Miss Little's love was true and steadfast and Alice was nothing but a flirt.

Miss Little patted Alice's arm.

'No, I suppose I haven't. I turned down other offers because of it but sometimes wonder what could have happened if I took a second chance at happiness.

'Don't let me force you into writing to your young man back where you came from if you feel you are settling here and there may be another choice for you.'

Miss Little had the kind of eyes that made you think she saw more than other people.

They parted outside the gate and went their different ways.

'Thank you, miss,' Alice called.

There was a shout after Alice as she began the walk home, happy to have experienced some of the interaction after church despite having to hurry back to Mrs Fleming. She felt content. She was someone whom people sought out in the church yard. Now she turned to see Ivy hurrying along after her.

'You weren't going to leave without talking to me, were you?' Ivy linked arms with Alice as if they were old friends.

'I have to hurry back. Mrs Fleming is ill.'

'So you could invite a friend for supper in the kitchen and she would never know.' Ivy laughed.

Alice wasn't sure if it was a serious suggestion or not.

'I would not like to be found entertaining someone if she got up to ask for something,' she said. 'It would not seem right.' She wanted to ask about Ivy's own arrangement for dinner — surely her mother would be planning something and Ivy would have to be there.

'It was in jest, you mouse. But I would like to see your house.'

Ivy held on to Alice's arm up to the turn off and there Alice unlinked her own, although Ivy seemed determined to cling to her.

'This is where I leave you,' Alice said.

'Let me see the house.' Ivy started to walk along the path until it opened out and the lodge was in front of them.

Alice wondered what it would look like in Ivy's eyes. It was not grand but large enough and its dimensions were pleasing.

She'd become used to the tangle of shrubs and trees all around and had begun to like seeing it as she returned home, the few times she had been out.

But now she felt uncomfortable because Ivy was such an exotic creature you couldn't predict what she would do next and, whether it made Alice a mouse or not, she was worried Ivy would do or say something outrageous in front of Mrs Fleming.

She held her breath as Ivy strode past the robins. She didn't know why but she wasn't going to risk pointing them out to Ivy.

The back door stood open and there were sounds from inside. Either the housekeeper was up and well or she'd come down for a drink.

'Mrs Fleming is there,' Alice whispered. 'I'm afraid you can't go in.'

'What a pity.' At least Ivy lowered her voice as she sidled up to the door. 'I just want to have a peep.'

Ivy glanced in. What would she have been able to see? The copper, the scrubbed table, the stairs up to the kitchen? This would not be of any interest to a girl who spent part of her life working in such a place.

'How do you get through to the hall and staircase?' Ivy asked.

'You can't go in, Ivy. Not with Mrs Fleming there.'

'I know, silly. I'm just interested.'

'You'd better go now.' Alice was so nervous.

Fortunately, Ivy turned and danced off. Alice resisted the temptation to go after her to make sure she left but watched and soon enough there was a flash of movement on the path down to the road and she was satisfied the girl had gone.

Well, perhaps it was understandable. Alice was quite keen to see Ivy's house, she had to admit. She still didn't know whether there were any other brothers or sisters or what Ivy's parents did.

Maybe next week she'd ask if she could see Ivy's home and find out more.

In the meantime, Alice checked on her robins every now and then, not every day because she was afraid to scare them off. First there was one egg and she celebrated. Then, a few days later, four eggs.

'They're early laying this year,' Mr Hopkin had told her. 'They lay one a day. Four may be their limit this time or there may be one or two more.'

'And then she sits on them?'

He nodded.

'We must be specially careful not to disturb them then. He will come and go, feeding her.'

Now there were pieces of broken eggshell around the nest and Alice could have cried. She waited impatiently for Mr Hopkin to arrive.

'Mr Hopkin,' she began, without any greeting and without taking the baskets. 'There are pieces of broken eggshell where our robins live. Could one have fallen from the nest?'

'It's more likely they're starting to hatch. Where were we when we first saw the nest? Two weeks into Lent? And now Passiontide is almost upon us. It is time for them to hatch. As they move around the nest fragments of shell would be pushed out.'

'Oh, I hope it's only that. I was so afraid. Will they leave soon?'

'The parents look after the little ones for a good few weeks more while they grow their feathers and learn to fly.'

'That's good.' She looked up to the

overhanging branches blocking the view of the open sky and wondered what it would feel like to fly.

* * *

One day towards the end of the week, as Alice made her way into the scullery after cleaning the upstairs rooms, she heard voices at the back door, two male voices, but when she opened it only one man stood there. Small and shabby, he could have been forty or fifty and his skin looked grey and unhealthy.

The man stood there for a moment. Could this be the knife grinder Mrs Fleming had mentioned might call and he'd had to leave his instruments at the end of the side alley?

'Can I help you?'

The man looked to the side along the path he must have come down.

'I've had a long walk and wonder if I might trouble you for a drop of water?'

Alice nodded and turned to get it for him. As she poured and pondered whether there might be something she could give him to eat she realised he'd followed her in.

He drank the water, his small eyes looking all round him.

Alice tore off a hunk of bread.

'Take this but you must leave. The housekeeper will be down any minute.'

'It's just you and the housekeeper, then, looking after her ladyship?'

'Of course not.' Alice felt uneasy with this man in her scullery. If he'd just arrived in the village after a long journey that would not be a normal sort of question to ask and why would he talk of her ladyship?

He must have listened to talk in the village where people called Mrs Younger Lady Eleanor.

'Why would you think so?' she challenged.

There was no answer. She found an apple for him and pushed him towards the door.

'You must leave before my mistress's brother gets back with his men. Take this for your journey.'

The man hesitated, then made his way up the side path. Alice knew she was right not to trust him. A hungry traveller would not have entered without leave and would at least have thanked her for the food and drink.

More, a hungry traveller would not have left the main thoroughfare to come to this isolated house at all.

As he disappeared around to the front of the house, Alice slipped out to follow him. She'd been right. There were two male voices.

'Sir Edward there?' The other man's voice was younger, but it was sneering and ugly. 'Or did you let yourself be fooled by the pretty little housemaid?'

The voices faded as the men drew away and Alice dared not risk showing herself even to get a look at the other man.

She could have told him there was nothing worth stealing. Her mistress had brought no jewellery and the silver and plate they'd found in the house was not of the best quality.

Alice went back to her work, firmly locking the door behind her.

'The mistress wants to go to the church service tomorrow morning,' Mrs Fleming told Alice on the Saturday. 'I think you should come with us.'

There was a room that was little more than an alcove off the kitchen that Mrs Fleming had made her own where she did the necessary paperwork and kept the orders and receipts.

It wasn't as nice as the room Mrs Fleming had at Mr Younger's house, where she would invite the butler for their daily conferences — when it was rumoured they sometimes drank a glass of sherry — but it served its purpose. It was in there that Alice had stammered out the story of the unwelcome visitor and there that Mrs Fleming called her now.

'Sit down, Alice.'

This was unheard of. Alice perched gingerly on the edge of a chair on the other side of the desk. It was true Mrs

Fleming had scolded her less since her scare of the other morning but as the weeks wore on the housekeeper seemed altogether more weary and less enthusiastic about the situation they were in.

Mrs Fleming sighed.

'Mrs Younger sees that this situation cannot continue for long. Three women alone in a household like this was bound to provoke talk but I hadn't considered the danger. Mrs Younger sees that she needs to show herself to gain respect but she's — well, she's not Miss Little.'

What did that mean?

'No, Mrs Fleming.'

Alice thought her voice must have sounded doubtful because Mrs Fleming went on to explain.

'Miss Little grew up in this village. It's hard to fit in as a new arrival.'

'Yes, Mrs Fleming.' That at least Alice could agree with.

'Mrs Younger has agreed to send for her brother to call again to discuss — what to do next.' Mrs Fleming sighed.

'And Sunday?'

'Ah, yes, Sunday. Mrs Younger and I are invited back to Miss Little's after the service. We'll lock the doors as best we can but if anyone sees the Lord's day as an opportunity to steal I don't want them to find you here on your own. I've spoken to the smallholder's wife and you will go to them after the service.'

Mrs Fleming concerned about her welfare? This was a surprise.

'Now,' Mrs Fleming went on, 'Miss Little's maid is ill, or her mother is.' Mrs Fleming seemed uncharacteristically flustered. 'She can't go in for a few days anyway. Alice . . . '

Alice knew what was coming and was surprised Mrs Fleming didn't just come out and say it. This was the woman who had hurried her out of the only home she knew in the middle of the night and put her down somewhere else for her to make her way. Why was it difficult to tell Alice she'd promised her to some-one else? A second house to clean in the same number of daylight hours.

Still, Alice liked Miss Little and it

would help Ivy and her family, too.

'If the mistress can spare me, I could go along to Miss Little's, Mrs Fleming.'

If everything was going to change once Sir Edward came back to hector his sister back home, Alice would at least know more of the world before she left, even if it was just one more house in one street in one village.

A Perfect Day

Miss Little was waiting for them outside the church and they all walked in together. Alice held back but Miss Little ushered her down the aisle and stood aside to nod her into the pew first.

This was even further forward than where the Hopkins sat. You had a whole different view of the service and there was much less to distract you.

Alice jumped when she saw Daniel standing by the church gate as they came slowly out. Surely he wasn't waiting for her?

'Good morning,' he greeted them all.

Mrs Fleming responded but Alice noted the mistress barely acknowledged him — too far below her, Alice assumed. Miss Little, it seemed, was never without a kind word regardless of position.

'Did Mrs Fleming ask you to come and fetch me?' Alice asked when they had all turned to go their separate ways. She wanted to believe he cared for her but it was possible the housekeeper had paid him. As if she were a parcel to be packaged up and sent from place to place with no say in the matter.

'No. Pa and I agreed we didn't want you to have to walk alone.'

Alice nodded. That would have to do. She didn't remember her own father but how different her life would have been if she'd had a father like Mr Hopkin.

'Your pa has always been kind to me,' Alice said. 'As have you, Daniel.'

He smiled and held her gaze until Alice tripped again while looking into those clear eyes.

She laughed.

'It's a good thing you take such care of me. I can't walk without tripping up.'

'I can't ask you to take my arm with so many people around.' Daniel laughed as well. He walked a little closer for a moment so their arms touched. 'But maybe on the way home.'

She smiled. It wouldn't happen, though. She was prepared to have to leave early so that the family could go to the afternoon service and they would all walk together and drop her at the lodge. Or if they persuaded Alice to go to church again with them, Ivy would be there and they'd all have to walk back past the lodge in any case. But Alice resolved to enjoy her day and not worry about how it would end.

Maggie came to the door to greet them.

'Did you see Mrs Younger, Daniel? What does she look like? Nobody told me to notice the last time she was at church.'

'I didn't notice this time either,' Daniel said. 'She had a bonnet on.'

'Grrr. You'll tell me, won't you, Alice? Is she beautiful?'

Alice hesitated. It had never occurred to her to wonder if her mistress was beautiful.

'There,' Daniel said. 'That means she's not and Alice doesn't want to say so.'

'She hasn't brought her fine clothes and jewels here, Maggie, if you were hoping to see them,' Alice said. 'She probably looks quite ordinary.'

'Did she often go to balls?' Maggie asked. 'Before?'

'Not often.'

Mrs Hopkin was in the kitchen.

'Maggie has been longing to know more about your poor mistress,' she said as they all crowded in.

'Why poor?' Maggie demanded.

'You know why.' Her mother looked reprovingly at her and then back at Alice. 'I keep thinking the news from the palace must make her more unhappy.'

'News?' Alice asked. 'We don't hear any news. At least, not that anyone tells me.'

'The Queen has not long had another child.'

Alice was confused.

'And Mrs Younger hasn't had any babies,' Maggie told Alice gently. 'Ma, do you think Miss Little is sad as well? Because she didn't have babies.'

'No, I don't think so, Maggie. There is more than one way for women to live happily. Mrs Younger must find her own way.'

'Is it true what they say?' Alice asked. 'That the Queen married for love?' Alice had been at her aunt's and remembered hearing a lot of talk about Victoria and Albert at the time of the royal wedding.

Mrs Hopkin smiled.

'So they say.'

Alice had a feeling she had as well and she was certain the quiet farmer loved his wife and his family.

'We supposed Mrs Younger must have done the same when she married,' Mrs Hopkin went on. 'People said it wouldn't work because he was so far below her. I'd be sorry if it turned out to be true that the difference in rank is making her unhappy.'

'Mr Younger seems very grand to me,' Alice said, remembering the times when he would engage musicians to come and play of an evening when he had friends or business acquaintances to visit.

The mistress always seemed to smile on those occasions.

'Alice,' Maggie interrupted her thoughts,

'you must come and see the nook I've made for myself in the barn.'

'Don't go,' Daniel said. 'Maggie reads the most ghastly books in there and anyone who agrees to see it has to read them to her while she lies on her back in the straw.'

'Let Maggie enjoy her books while she can,' their mother said. 'She doesn't believe me but there will be no lying on her back dreaming up at the big house.'

'Is it next week you go? How far is it?'

'Yes,' Daniel said. 'It's about five or six miles, I'd say.'

'It's a pity he didn't stay in his father's house in the park behind the lodge,' Mrs Hopkin said thoughtfully. 'Although they do say the new place is more modern.'

'What happened to the other house?' Alice asked.

'He sold it to be developed and made a lot of money — as if he didn't have enough already.'

'He did spend some of it on improvements in the village,' Daniel said.

'And some of it on chandeliers, by all

accounts.'

Alice was pleased the mistress's brother looked after his tenants, although she hoped Maggie would not have to clean the chandeliers. She turned to Maggie.

'At least you will be able to come back on your day off.' She had always envied the girls who had families to go to when they were allowed.

'Maggie imagines dressing in a pretty uniform and dusting books all day. She thinks they'll let her borrow their books.'

'They might,' Maggie insisted. 'Mightn't they, Alice?'

Alice hesitated.

'They may not have the kind of volumes you would like to read, Maggie. What do you like?'

'Ghost stories and mysteries and romances.' Maggie turned back to Alice, her voice dreamy. 'In my nook there's a gap in the roof where you can see the blue of the sky and sometimes a cloud. You can be anything when you're looking up at it.'

'I have a little window in my room,'

Alice told her. 'I can look across a long way and it makes me feel like that.'

'Come with me this afternoon and I'll read to you,' Maggie said. 'You must be so lonely.'

Alice began to fear less the change going into service was going to represent for Maggie when she was persuaded into the barn that afternoon. Alice had expected a sweet-smelling light-filled room but Maggie's nook turned out to be up a rickety ladder into a cramped draughty roof space where you couldn't stand up straight and you could only see the sky because the roof was broken.

How odd that Daniel repaired other people's roofs and his own gaped to the open air. Still, she could see this barn was small and little used. There was a larger, better used one further away and a solid-looking building Maggie told her was the dairy. Maggie was lucky her family allowed her some leisure time and let her read here.

'Lie on your back, Alice. I'll brush your dress as clean as new afterwards.'

'You'll miss this when you go up to the big house.'

'It's very cold here in the winter months,' Maggie said. 'I'll find somewhere warm in Sir Edward's place.'

'That's probably not the way it would happen, you know, Maggie, dear.' Alice saw she would need to be harsh to convince the young girl she wasn't going to be able to curl up in the mistress's brother's library whenever she felt like it. Or ever. 'They'll make you work very hard.'

'I know how to work hard, Alice. We have to keep everything spotless here, especially for the bread and jam making. Kneading bread is heavy work and I know how to make butter and cheese as well. You mustn't worry about me.'

'I worry it will feel very different without your family.'

'I make up stories in my head,' Maggie told her. 'I won't have time to feel lonely. Do you want to hear one?'

There wasn't much time to convince Maggie of the realities of the way her life would be. She would have to bring it up again later.

'All right.'

'It's about the lodge. There was a family living there many years ago and the daughter fell in love with a passing sailor.'

'Are we near the sea, then?'

'No. He ran away to sea when he was a boy because his father was cruel to him. He made his fortune and came home to the village.'

Alice settled back. It wasn't a true story, then. Maggie was making it up. She closed her eyes and was lulled by Maggie's soft voice telling of the way the daughter at the lodge fell madly in love with the sailor but that her parents wouldn't countenance the relationship.

It was a noise down below that disturbed Alice and she suddenly didn't know where she was.

The sailor had not returned from his latest journey and the daughter had fallen — from the roof? From a window? Alice hadn't heard properly. She must have been sleeping.

'And they say she still walks the passages of the lodge at night dressed all in white and looking for her love.'

'Maggie!' Daniel's head appeared at the top of the ladder and Alice started upright.

She had never seen Daniel angry.

'I told you not to frighten Alice with ghost stories. You'll make her afraid to be in that house.'

Maggie looked as shocked as Alice felt.

'I only meant to amuse her . . . '

'Not everybody finds being scared to death amusing.' Daniel glared at his sister. 'Remember you have your sisters to curl up between at night when you think of your ghosts and imagine they might be real. Alice doesn't have that advantage.' The glare turned to a look of exasperation. 'I came to say Ma wants you, Maggie. I just wish I'd arrived earlier.'

'Daniel, I . . . '

'Tell me later.'

Maggie nodded and Daniel went down the ladder to allow her to make her escape.

Alice still felt shaken by the unexpect-edness of Daniel's anger but it seemed to fade as quickly as it came.

She couldn't hear any more words exchanged down below so assumed the two had gone back to the house together. It was gratifying that Daniel had been so thoughtful of her comfort again but he'd gone and left her here without a word. Maybe his mother needed him for some-thing as well.

She prepared herself to make her way down when a swish of movement told her he was coming back up.

'I'm sorry my sister is so thoughtless,' he said, settling himself where Maggie had sat. 'I should have remembered to tell you to stop her if there were ghosts in her story.'

'The ghost didn't come until the very end.' Alice laughed. 'I thought it was a romance.'

'A lord and a farmer's daughter?' Dan-iel laughed too.

'No, a sailor and the daughter at the

lodge.'

'A sailor, eh? She must have got that idea from one of the books she's read. The man is usually much higher in station but can't resist the beautiful girl, despite the rags she dresses in. Do all girls have the same idea?'

'No, but sometimes when a handsome young visitor came to the house a couple of the maids would start to imagine if he had a glimpse of them he would fall in love with them and take them away from their life of hard work.'

'Not you?' Daniel looked at Alice with interest. It was so different sitting here with Daniel. Just as comfortable as she'd been with Maggie but there was a warmth in her chest and excitement in her stomach. Being close to Daniel, she would not have nodded off during the story. He made her feel too alive.

'I kept my eyes down,' she answered. 'I don't like the thought of having to go to balls and endless dinners. And I'd feel so sorry for the maids who had to look after me I'd want to help them with their work!'

Alice couldn't make out Daniel's expression in the dappled light of the barn. He was smiling at her but there was something else she couldn't identify. Perhaps he thought her foolish and unambitious.

'I don't suppose the sailor would have gone to many balls,' he said after a while.

'He'd made his fortune at sea,' Alice told him. 'He was no ordinary sailor.'

Daniel laughed again.

'Of course not.' Then he became serious again. 'My parents worry that Maggie will be too dreamy to be a maid. I hope she finds herself among dreamers who want lords to fall in love with them. She can make up endless tales to keep them amused.'

Perhaps he pitied her for her lack of imagination in comparison to his sister. He may even have dreams of his own.

'And a lady catching the eye of a farmer's son?' she asked. 'Does Maggie tell this story, too?'

'Not in my hearing. She thinks me far too dull to consider such a thing.'

Mr Hopkin came into the barn, coughing and making more noise than necessary, making his presence felt.

'Who thinks you dull?' His head appeared at the top of the ladder.

'Maggie.'

'Ah, Maggie. She thinks us all dull. We are all needed downstairs, dull or interesting — there are hens to feed, cheese to stir, eggs to collect.' He disappeared down the ladder. 'Alice may choose what she wants to do but it looks like her holiday is over.'

There was no rancour between the brother and sister after Daniel lost his temper with Maggie and Maggie was in no way cowed. Alice was warmly encouraged to go with them to the afternoon church service and she felt more and more comfortable with them all.

Her aunt, Alice recalled, had frowned for hours if the young Alice ever did anything to displease her. It was a rare enough occurrence — Alice was a compliant being and always anxious to please.

Charlie too, she reflected, could

remain in a bad mood for a long time. If she couldn't get away to meet him he would often spoil the next occasion by still being upset with her. She liked Daniel's way of being much better.

'Ivy wasn't at the morning service, either,' Alice commented to the family on the way out of the churchyard.

She didn't know why she kept bringing this name into the conversation but it always happened. She wanted to see the reaction, she supposed.

'Her mother must be bad,' Mrs Hopkin said.

They reached the place where the road up to the lodge met the main street and Alice stopped. It was too late to ask any more, though she still needed to know what position Ivy played in this family — and in Daniel's heart.

For a second her breath caught in her throat. Was this why Daniel was always talking about Charlie? To find out whether he still meant anything to Alice?

She turned to Mrs Hopkin.

'Thank you for such a nice day.'

'You're welcome, Alice.' There was warmth in her voice. 'Daniel, walk Alice up to her door. Maggie is dawdling behind; I'll send her after you so she can say goodbye to Alice. We don't know if she will be able to come back next Sunday or not.'

And now Daniel was looking at her and expecting her to walk with him. The few score steps to the side of the house were passed in silence and Alice wondered if Daniel didn't know how to break the silence either or if he was anxious not to talk. Perhaps it bothered him to hear Ivy's name on her lips. It was supposed to be secret after all.

'My uncle and I are taking Maggie up to Sir Edward's house early in the morning,' Daniel told her. 'Then we are going on to work on some houses in a village beyond Sir Edward's place.' He looked at her.

'It's only repairs, not a full roof, but I'm not sure how long I'm going to be away.'

Alice nodded, her heart sinking.

'Your mother will be sorry to be without two of her children.'

'And you?'

Alice stopped walking as they reached the solidness of the side wall and they stood face to face for a moment. Alice's breath grew short.

'I will miss Maggie as well. And I will think about you every moment you are away and wish you safe and God speed home when your work is done.'

He didn't take his eyes off of her.

'I will like to think of you thinking of me.'

It would have been easy to turn her face up to let him kiss her. Alice wanted it more than she ever wanted to be close to Charlie, but his family were not far away and Maggie would arrive any second. One of them had to break the spell.

'We must walk carefully past my robins,' Alice said, moving on slowly. 'The chicks have hatched and are busy growing feathers.'

'Your robins?' He smiled and caught her eye again.

Alice's heart soared. He may or may not be promised to Ivy but Alice's senses raced when he looked at her like that and he felt it too, she was certain of it.

'I'm sure it's the one I heard calling on my first day here,' she said softly. 'Then your father pointed out where they were building their nest and we saw the newly laid eggs and then the chicks. I feel responsible for them.'

She crept past the nest, not even looking, fearful of disturbing the occupants.

Daniel caught her arm once they were both past.

'Alice, you're . . . ' He heard a noise behind them and moved swiftly back the way they'd come to stop Maggie careening down the path and disturbing the wildlife.

She came more quietly forward and Alice kissed and hugged her goodbye.

'I expect I'll see you next week,' Maggie said.

'It's Easter next week,' Alice said.

'So they'll give us all time off to visit our families,' the girl said confidently.

'They may well have visitors and there will be extra work. Don't be sad if it's longer before you can get home.'

Alice could see Daniel behind Maggie shaking his head rather sadly. She wasn't going to be convinced and Alice just hoped it was not going to be too difficult for Maggie to learn the truth.

But how wonderful she and Daniel were thinking the same thing. What was he going to tell her she was when he said, 'Alice, you're . . . ? And would he have kissed her if she hadn't lost her nerve and started talking?'

At Miss Little's

Just for a moment as she rang Miss Little's bell, there being no way round to the back in this neat little terrace, Alice was afraid she'd misunderstood and it would be Ivy who opened the door to her, blonde tresses constricted under a cap. That wouldn't have felt right. But it was a middle-aged woman in a brown dress and with a welcoming smile.

'Come along in, Miss Little's expecting you,' the woman said. 'She's in there.' She pointed to a door on the left. 'And the kitchen's that way. Come down when you're ready.' She knocked at the door and opened it following a muffled reply. 'In you go.'

At least no-one announced her, the way the footman would at the house she'd been in before. And at least Miss Little didn't get up to walk across the floor to greet her the way she'd seen Mr Younger do sometimes when she'd been with another girl setting tea out. Mrs

Younger didn't ever do that, not that she'd seen. Maybe only men did. Either way, Alice was not important enough for anyone to do that.

And while all this was going through Alice's head she was taking in the room, small but elegant and welcoming, with one wall filled with bookshelves, a cosy arrangement of chairs and sofas by the fireplace and a big desk that Miss Little was seated behind.

'Alice. It's good of you to come.'

What was the right answer to that? It was good of you to ask me? But she still didn't know exactly why she was here.

'I hope I'll be of some use.'

'I'm sure you will. I need someone to help with some sweeping and whatever my cook needs assistance with while Ivy is occupied with her family. As you see, this is not a large house. Not what you're used to.'

'No, Miss Little.' Unless the rest of it had been badly neglected this house would not be so hard to keep clean as the lodge house with its dark corners —

or Mr Younger's big house with its four floors and two staircases.

And surely Miss Little's pots would not be numerous to scrub. Little suited her as a name. She probably didn't eat four meals a day and five courses at dinner.

Miss Little continued looking at Alice.

'Ivy isn't ill, is she, miss?' Alice ventured.

Miss Little shook her head.

'It's her mother and she says the smaller children need to be looked after.'

'That's very difficult for Ivy.'

Miss Little gave a small smile.

'Perhaps.'

Alice glanced down and saw a number of big boxes on her side of the desk.

Miss Little chuckled.

'I see you've spotted all my other books and papers. If we get on all right and it's not too much for you I'm going to ask Lady Eleanor if she can continue to spare you after Ivy is back to help me organise them.'

Alice shook her head in panic. She

didn't want to let Miss Little down.

'I don't think I'll be very good with papers.'

'Do not be concerned, my dear. I won't ask you to do anything you're not capable of.' Miss Little smiled. 'I think you'll get on very well.' She nodded. 'Now. My cook will answer any questions you have about that side of the work but is there anything else you want to ask me?'

Alice stood up, recognising she was being dismissed.

'Why does everyone here call Mrs Younger Lady Eleanor?'

'When she lived with her parents and brother at the big house when it was in the park behind your lodge, that's the name she was always known by, just like her brother was always a Lord because of his parents but gained a knighthood in his own right a few years ago. Because her husband is only a Mr, Eleanor can't continue to use her title.'

Yes, this is what Mrs Hopkin had said, her mistress married someone below her in rank. If she'd married for love, her love hadn't lasted. Or she'd made a mistake. She shouldn't have to suffer because of that. It was easy to make mistakes.

But now wasn't the time to talk or think of that. Now, she had to make her way to the kitchen to learn about the work in this house.

★ ★ ★

On Wednesday Miss Little called Alice in to her office, where she had opened some of the boxes. There were pencils and sheets of paper on the desk.

'I'm going to put these into order,' she told Alice. 'Tell me, did you learn how to form your letters at all?'

Alice's stomach felt heavy.

'A little. But I don't remember.' There may have been Sunday school lessons while her mother lived and her aunt had tried to teach her, but mostly what she learned was sewing. She was very good at stitching but Alice feared her letters were forgotten.

'Never mind. We'll take it slowly. I'll

just write some letters here.' Miss Little took one page and made a large 'A' on it. Alice recognised that one. Then Miss Little wrote on a second and third page. 'That's 'E',' she said. 'And that's an 'I'.' Now, when I give you one of my letters I want you to copy the letter I say on to the envelope, or the top of the letter if there is no envelope, and place it under the right page.'

Alice could hear her pulse beating. This didn't sound very complicated but she was already flustered.

'This one is an 'A',' Miss Little said.

Alice took up a pencil and carefully marked it with the same letter. That wasn't so hard. She did remember once being able to write her own name and this was the first letter.

'Splendid. And so is this one.'

It got easier with practice. After a while Miss Little suggested adding two more letters, and so by the end of the afternoon Alice could once again confidently write her name and also, Miss Little pointed out 'lie', 'lace' and 'ice'.

She even got Alice to write them out for her.

'Let's continue tomorrow. I think we're going to get on splendidly.'

Alice hurried home and felt confident enough to peer at her robins. They would be taking it in turns, Mr Hopkin had told her, to feed the hungry chicks.

'Who's there?' Mrs Fleming appeared with a copper pan in her hand, peering as if alarmed at her.

'Mrs Fleming, it's me, Alice. Whatever has happened?'

'Oh. Alice. Someone has broken in.'

Alice gasped.

'Did they take anything?'

'The mistress is looking but everything is turned all about.'

'Were you both here when it happened?'

'I persuaded Mrs Younger to take a turn about the village. It has been so wet lately and it seemed dry underfoot today. I thought she should get out.'

'Yes.' Alice was impressed that the housekeeper had been willing to tackle intruders with only a pot, albeit a large one, in her hands but she had never seen Mrs Fleming so much at a loss.

'If only I hadn't suggested it,' Mrs Fleming went on, going back into the scullery.

'Well, perhaps it is as well you weren't here when it happened.'

'I suspect they were watching us, Alice.' Now the housekeeper's face was grim. 'I don't know where from but watching us somehow. They were quick. We didn't go far. The front door was wide open when we returned.'

'They broke in the front door?'

'I'm sure we didn't leave it open.' But Mrs Fleming didn't seem sure. 'I was just checking the kitchenware and the back door had not been touched. Then I thought someone was loitering outside.' She stepped up into the kitchen. 'Some of the servers are silver but none of them seem to have been taken.'

Alice checked with her and everything seemed in order.

'Mrs Fleming, was there anything in particular, do you think, they were looking for?'

'What do you mean?'

'People have asked me about the mistress's jewellery, as if they knew there was something valuable.'

'People?'

'Chatting after church.'

'What have you told them?' Mrs Fleming was standing still now, looking at Alice.

'I've always said she didn't bring any jewellery with her,' Alice said. 'I clean and tidy, you see, as you know, and I've never seen any. Was I wrong to say so?'

'Not at all. But they clearly didn't believe it.'

She thought for a moment and Alice was afraid the housekeeper was going to ask who Alice had said this to.

'The trouble is this village is such a place for tittle-tattle any sort of rumour could have got around. Now, I need to go out for a few minutes. I'm sure nothing else will happen today but keep the doors locked just in case. Just some cold cuts and potatoes tonight, I think, Alice,

114

if you could, please.'

Mrs Fleming was back in control.

Alice tried to recover her happiness that she was beginning to learn to read but it was difficult. She had a feeling this happiness was going to be whisked away from her.

★ ★ ★

Alice was scrubbing the pots after breakfast the next morning when she heard a commotion at the front door. Alice was looking forward to finishing her chores here and going to Miss Little's.

To learn to read! She spared a thought for Maggie, starting her fourth day at the big house and possibly still bewildered. But Maggie had the strong pull of her family in the district and Alice knew she would see her again. She would borrow books from Maggie. They could read together.

And she would finally write to Charlie to tell him she had met someone else and she hoped he had as well. She was feeling confident again. Every day that passed brought her nearer to the day Daniel would finish the roofs and come home.

She'd make sure they made time to talk properly, whatever the outcome was. Then at least she'd know. She had no doubt he would be easier to talk to than Charlie ever was.

Hearing the noise at the front door, Alice took one of the pans and crept along the hallway to see what was happening. She didn't think burglars would knock at the front door and announce themselves but seeing Mrs Fleming so nervous yesterday made her cautious.

A voice Alice thought she recognised was speaking in polite and measured tones.

'Wait while you prepare yourself. Your husband was anxious we set off as soon as possible.'

The mistress's voice, in contrast, was high-pitched and agitated.

'So anxious to have me home that he sent his steward to fetch me.'

Ah, that's who it was — Mr Baxter, Mr Younger's steward. She'd served him tea sometimes when there was business to be discussed.

'He has a pressing engagement this morning but will be there to welcome you home when we arrive, I am certain.'

'He may be there, sir, but I will not. Now I must ask you again to leave.'

Alice went back to the scullery as the argument continued. She was afraid the mistress wasn't going to win and Alice needed to think. Mrs Fleming had been standing behind the mistress, but it must have been she who sent for Mr Younger.

That must have been where she went yesterday, to get a message to her mistress's husband.

Alice jumped when she got back to the scullery to see a young man standing there. He was dressed in livery and logic told her this was a footman attending the steward but Alice lifted the copper pot in readiness.

The man put up both hands to fend her off.

117

'Alice! It is Alice, isn't it? I'm from Mr Younger's household. I'm the new foot-man.'

Alice lowered the pan. If you were going to steal from a house you wouldn't dress in livery and announce yourself.

The footman reached for something in his pocket.

'I've brought you this.'

There in neat letters on an envelope was written 'Alice'.

'Now I must hurry as the coachman and I need to find somewhere to see to the horses.' He turned at the doorway. 'This is a lonely place they've brought you to, Alice. I hope you'll be home soon.'

Home. Just as this village was begin-ning to feel like home they were going to package her up again and send her back.

She put the letter in her pocket and returned to the hall where Mr Baxter had still not managed to gain entry or persuade Mrs Younger to begin pack-ing. But the mistress was silent now and

Alice didn't think she would hold out much longer.

'Mrs Fleming,' she whispered and the housekeeper turned and stepped back. She looked so tired.

'I must run to Miss Little for a moment, to tell her I will be late.'

'That's all right, Alice. We will explain to Miss Little. She'll understand.'

'I would like her to know. She will be expecting me. It will only take a minute.'

Mrs Fleming had a sense of duty. She had let Alice go to church of a Sunday and now it looked as though she saw the rightness of keeping Miss Little informed. She nodded.

'Thank you, Mrs Fleming.'

Alice felt for the letter in her pocket and flew.

$$Moving Again

This time Alice had been sure it would be the pleasant cook who opened the door so she was shocked to see Ivy, and more shocked to see how displeased Ivy looked.

'How is your mother?'

119

'My mother is all right so Miss Little won't be needing you. The cook was going to tell you on her way back from picking up the bread.' Ivy wasn't standing back to let Alice in. 'I thought it was her at the door.'

'I need to see Miss Little just for a minute, Ivy. Could you let me in and tell her?'

'The mistress is occupied.'

'She'll see me for a minute, I'm sure of it.' She had been the one to offer to read a letter to Alice and to help her with her writing. Miss Little would be pleased to see Alice with a letter.

If the letter was from Charlie Alice needed to know what he said before she got in the carriage to go back.

The cook panted up behind Alice at the same time as Miss Little came out of her front parlour where her office was set up.

'There you are,' the cook said to Alice, breathing heavily. 'What a to-do at your place this morning.'

'Thank you, Ivy. You can get back to

your work now,' Miss Little said. 'Come in, Alice.'

Alice averted her eyes because she could see Ivy hated to be sent away while Alice was admitted. Surely they should have been exchanging friendly glances.

'Now, what is happening at Alice's place?'

'Mr Younger has sent someone to take my mistress back,' Alice explained.

'Yes,' the cook said. 'The talk in the village is of that but now another carriage has arrived and it looks like Sir Edward is there as well.'

'Poor Mrs Younger, being bullied by so many men. Come into my office, Alice.' Miss Little turned to her cook. 'I wonder if you could ask Ivy to bring us in some tea, please?'

'I will, miss.' The cook trundled down to the kitchen still breathless from hurrying and, Alice thought, the excitement of the morning.

Her own heart felt heavy as she followed Miss Little. Mrs Younger would not resist the combined efforts of her husband's emissary and her brother.

'I shouldn't stay, Miss Little,' Alice said. Surely the tea wasn't for her anyway. 'I expect we'll be leaving.'

Miss Little motioned to her to sit down and sat opposite. She was silent for a moment.

'That will be a pity.'

Alice drew out her letter.

'The footman who came with Mr Younger's steward brought this for me.'

Miss Little beamed.

'And you want to know what it says?'

Alice nodded and handed it over.

Miss Little opened the envelope and drew out two sheets of notepaper. She looked first at the end.

'It's from someone who signs herself 'Betty'. Do you know who that is?'

'Oh — not Charlie, then. I thought for so long if anyone wrote it would be him. Yes, I know Betty. She's a good friend, from the other house.' Alice thought for a moment. Yes, it made sense that it was Betty who would have written.

Miss Little cocked her head as though

listening for something and lifted a finger to warn Alice to be quiet. After a moment there was a knock at the door and Ivy came in with a tray of tea.

Miss Little tucked Alice's letter under her own papers out of sight before the girl got to the desk.

'Thank you, Ivy. That will be all.'

Ivy didn't smile or bob a curtsey or look at either Miss Little or Alice.

'I'd be sorry if you couldn't continue with the ordering of the papers, Alice.' Miss Little got up and walked across the room as she spoke. 'We got a lot done yesterday.' She opened the door and looked out.

It was almost as though she was accustomed to Ivy listening at the door. What on earth of interest could Ivy hope to find out and how uncomfortable for Miss Little not to be able to trust her servant. Alice was sorry she wouldn't be staying so she could warn Ivy to be careful not to lose her job over it.

'Now, where were we?' Miss Little poured tea then sat down and took the letter out. She nodded across to Alice.

'Drink your tea. This is what Betty says . . .

"Dear Alice, Everybody is saying they are going in the morning to bring Mrs Younger back and Mr Younger says he will have you back as well but not Mrs Fleming. He blames Mrs Fleming but not you but there is a new house-maid, she's called Susan, so I don't know what will happen.

'What I want to tell you about is that Charlie is now with Polly the parlour maid. I did not want to tell you before but I saw him kissing Polly in the garden before you went so you can't trust Charlie. I don't want you to be taken by surprise. I am going to try to get Frederic the new footman who is very nice to agree to bring this to you and Janet is writing it for me. Janet and I hope to see you tomorrow. Yours, Betty'.'

Alice had sat breathless while listening to this, imagining Betty getting everything out in a rush and Janet, who assisted the cook, trying to get it all down and wanting to add her own words.

Alice was pleased Betty had a new friend and someone to confide in. There was no point in wanting people to miss you if it made them unhappy. And she didn't have to worry about Charlie any more. She'd thought she didn't but it was a relief to have it confirmed.

'Well, at least you know.' Miss Little folded the letter up and tucked it back into the envelope. She looked carefully at Alice. 'Is it bad news?'

Alice shook her head.

'Good news. I was so worried I'd got it wrong. Charlie was so insistent I couldn't think straight until I got away but then I knew we weren't right for one another. Then I met . . . then I got very confused.'

'The heart knows, Alice. Even at my great age I get confused from time to time and find myself wondering if I should have married someone else, but I've had a happy independent life that

I might not have had if I'd married someone who wasn't right for me.' She nodded, her eye still on Alice. 'The heart knows.'

'And if the person you love loves someone else?'

Miss Little started as if the question took her by surprise.

'Then you want what's best for him, of course, but don't believe gossip. Hear it from him before you give up.'

That was as close to admitting it was Daniel her heart sought as Alice was going to come and you never knew whether Ivy was outside listening. Besides, why would someone like Miss Little know what someone like Daniel wanted?

'Could I ask one last favour, Miss Little?'

'I hope it's not the last, but do ask.'

She hesitated. It would be too obvious if she asked for Daniel's address. She wasn't ready to open her heart so completely. Miss Little would help her find another way.

'Could you write me down your address and if I manage to write a letter could you pass it on? If it's to someone close by?'

'Janet might be willing to help you, too.' Miss Little drew out two or three sheets of paper, folded them and put them into an envelope, on which she began to write in a firm hand. Alice recognised L and I and then L and E. Those two in between must be Ts. She felt an impatience to learn more words and letters. When was that going to happen now?

* * *

The two envelopes were tucked safely at the bottom of Alice's trunk, her clothes neatly folded on top. She wondered if the new footman, Frederic, would carry it down for her.

All was quiet downstairs. Alice made her way down. Perhaps they weren't leaving after all.

Mrs Fleming was standing in the

scullery, doing nothing.

'This is a muddle, Alice.'

She looked around the room. It was as tidy as it had ever been so it clearly wasn't the surroundings the housekeeper was talking about.

'Mr Baxter is about to depart,' Mrs Fleming went on, 'and I think you had better go with him. Mrs Younger is refusing to go unless her husband comes to get her so she and I will go to Sir Edward's.'

So perhaps Betty had got it wrong about Mrs Fleming not being allowed to return. Or no-one had told Mrs Fleming?

'Could I not go with you there?' Alice asked. Sir Edward's place was only six miles from Daniel. If only Alice could establish herself there she wouldn't need to go back when Mrs Younger did.

'You could if it wasn't that it was Easter. There would certainly be a place for you next week, he says. But Sir Edward has a house full for a couple of days and there will be no room for any of us until Monday or Tuesday.'

There was a gasp of surprise and Alice saw that the laundress had come in. Oh, dear. They'd forgotten to tell her they would not be needing her services this week and the poor woman had enough to do without a wasted journey.

'No room for his own sister,' the woman said, obviously disgusted. 'I've never heard of such a thing.'

Mrs Fleming turned to her.

'Ah, Violet. Well, it's short notice. He's offered to put us up at an inn.'

It must have been a surprise to Mrs Fleming as well to hear the laundry woman's comments. Mrs Fleming wouldn't make excuses for Sir Edward otherwise.

But Violet snorted at the explanation.

'But not the young soul who's worked her fingers to the bone for his sister.'

Mrs Fleming looked at Alice.

'I suppose you could sleep on the floor in my room.' She looked doubtful. 'And you may be able to help out somewhere in the inn.' She moved to the kitchen door and seemed to be looking to see if there was anyone still in the hall.

'Heaven forbid that you should be allowed to droop on a chair with her ladyship for three days,' Violet muttered.

Alice smothered her laughter.

'I'd rather sleep on your floor and do your sewing for you until Sir Edward's ready for me,' she said in an aside to the laundress. It was really too bad that just as she'd decided she had to stand up for herself things got worse.

But Violet had no qualms about speaking up.

'That's the ticket,' she said in a loud voice. 'We'll do that then, Mrs Fleming.' Violet bustled through the kitchen.

'No need for you to be on the floor,' she told Alice as she went. 'You can have my Stan's bed and he can make do. I'll send him round for your trunk.' She raised her voice again. 'Mrs Fleming, we've had a better idea . . .'

And so later Alice tried to quell her rising panic as she scurried beside Stanley, who had her trunk on his shoulder

130

and was striding along.

All of Alice's possessions and it was as if they were nothing.

And she so slow and dull she still wasn't sure what was happening. It had been her idea and she wasn't clear what this plan involved.

'Somebody will come and get you,' Mrs Fleming had said vaguely.

'You'll be all right with us, Alice,' Stanley said.

It was as if he recognised her doubt. What a sensitive young man for all his size. Alice wanted to say she was sorry his mother was turning him out of his bed for her but she had no idea what their house was like. Suppose there were beetles and rats on the floor at night? That would be miserable and she didn't want to volunteer to sleep there if she didn't have to.

'Is it much further?' They'd gone past the church, past Miss Little's, and the number of houses was dwindling.

She'd been hoping for the chance one day to run down to the Hopkins' but that was in the other direction. Mrs Fleming didn't let her go this morning because she'd already been to tell them the lodge wouldn't need any more deliveries, she told Alice. Alice wondered when she'd done that. But she needed to see them herself, one last time.

Unless she was sent to Sir Edward's and allowed to stay there. Then she might be able to come to visit some Sundays.

Oh, Mrs Fleming had been right that morning — it was all such a muddle. It was bad enough that Daniel was away for she didn't know how long, now she was being sent away as well.

'Sorry, Alice. Do you want to stop to rest?'

'You walk so fast.'

Stanley laughed.

'I forget how long my legs are.' He slowed his pace. 'We're nearly there.'

They turned off the road towards a pair of cottages standing alone with a number of outbuildings between them. Steam was coming from one of them.

Stanley led Alice around the out-buildings and to the back of the smaller cottage.

'We're here, Ma,' he called.

A tall, well built young woman came out, wiping her brow with her left hand. Her right she held in front of her, wrapped in cotton wadding. This could be Stanley's sister. Alice hadn't considered there would be brothers or sisters.

'She has the flat irons going and doesn't want to stop but says to take Alice in,' the woman said, then looked at Alice. 'Hello. I'm Hetty, Stanley's brother's wife.' She lifted her bandaged hand. 'Thank you for agreeing to help us while I am having to work one-handed.'

Ah, this explained what Alice was doing here. Stanley hadn't mentioned that his sister-in-law helped in the business as well, or even that he had a brother. This was going to be a long couple of days if she wasn't going to be told what was going on.

Alice sighed and made her way into

the house. Just as she thought she was starting to see the light on things in her life, she was back in the dark again.

A Good Gossip

'Stop now if you'd like to.' Violet reached for another garment herself.

Alice stood up for a moment and stretched. She didn't think she'd ever spent so long at a time sitting down.

'I'll keep going too,' she said. 'It's satisfying to see the pile go down.'

'There will be more tomorrow.' Violet laughed. 'We're never finished.'

'It's good there's enough work to keep the whole family together,' Alice said.

'Stanley thinks they'll invent machines and we won't be needed soon enough.'

Alice had heard talk of the machines that were being invented for all manner of operations.

'I'm waiting for the one for scrubbing floors,' she said with a laugh. 'And pots.'

'They're called housemaids.'

Violet was much more fun than Alice would have thought, and more interesting, with a host of stories to tell about her own life and her neighbours'.

She'd started taking in washing many years before, she explained. Gradually her sons had started to help her and the business expanded and when the older boy married they were able to let him have the house and build a new, smaller one for Violet and Stanley, the younger son. Violet's strong daughter-in-law also started to help in the business and was a real asset.

The plan was to build another house nearby for Stanley when the time came.

Alice opened her mouth to say that Stanley would make someone a good husband one day when she decided against it. Suppose they got the idea she meant for herself?

So Alice opened her mouth but stopped herself from speaking and the breath caught in her throat and she started to choke. By the time Violet brought her some water she'd forgotten where they were in the conversation.

'And Ivy's family, what do you know

of them?' Alice asked as they settled back to their rhythmic work. 'Miss Little's maidservant? Stanley works for Miss Little sometimes, doesn't he? Does her mother ail?'

Violet looked over her shoulder, though Stanley was in his brother's house, where he was going to sleep.

'Ah, yes. Mary.' Violet looked wistful. 'We used to be good friends, me and Mary and Elizabeth, before we all got married.'

'Elizabeth?'

'You know her, Elizabeth Hopkin. Before she married Graham Hopkin. You know what young girls are like when they get together, dreaming of handsome young men and who they'll marry.' Violet laughed. 'We even had our children grown up and married to one another.'

'They're all similar ages, aren't they?'

'I married first and Mary a bit later and then Elizabeth met her Graham when I already had my first boy.' Violet stopped sewing for a moment and looked up at the mantelpiece. 'Then my man died of the summer sickness.'

'Oh, Violet, what a tragedy for you.'

'It was. Mary was expecting Ivy and I'd just found out I was expecting Stanley. We didn't see so much of Elizabeth by then because Graham had got the tenancy he works now but she was about to give birth to her first.'

'Daniel?'

'Yes. I had family about me and my mother was a saint.' She paused and smiled as if remembering. 'Around that time Ivy's father got into trouble. My husband had never liked him somehow. He was in . . . he had to go away for a while and Mary found it hard. We practically had Ivy living with us, to make sure she wasn't neglected.'

'That must have been hard, with your own little one and your grieving and all.' Alice liked Violet more and more.

'That was when I started taking washing in,' Violet went on. She laughed. 'It couldn't have been that healthy for the children, the air was wet all the time until we managed to do the barn out.' She laughed again. 'But it doesn't seem to have done Stanley much harm.'

Alice smiled.

'And you've carried on being a close family.' She remembered the talk of Ivy looking after younger children. 'Mary's husband came back?'

'He comes and goes. He's a bad influence on Ivy, and has friends who are a bad influence, that much I can see.'

'And Mary ails?'

Violet sighed.

'Mary does what she can. Money has always been a problem and only having daughters means there is less coming in. A boy she could have sent to do better paid work.'

Alice sensed there was more to come. She held her breath, not knowing what question to ask.

'Ivy was such a pretty little thing.' So Violet was focused on the past, not the present. 'I think both Elizabeth and I had ideas of her as a daughter-in-law at one time.'

So did that mean they didn't have those ideas now? 'She's still pretty, isn't she?'

'Is she? Well, it's not for me to say. I'd like my Stanley to marry someone hard working and reliable but they're all free to choose who they like. I don't know what young Ivy's about these days but she's trouble. Miss Little is goodness itself to keep her on.' Violet sighed and began to sort the mending into piles.

'We always said it was a good thing we weren't like the gentry, selling our children off to the highest bidder to make a good marriage.'

'Do you think that's what happened to Mrs Younger? Lady Eleanor, you would call her.'

Violet stopped what she was doing and her face softened.

'No. Not at all. Your Lady Eleanor married her common man for love, against the wishes of all her family.'

'Why do you think she's run away from him?'

'I'll tell you what Elizabeth Hopkin

140

thinks, and she's a woman who understands the human heart. She thinks because poor Eleanor hasn't had children yet she feels she's not fulfilling the promise she made to her John when they wed.'

Alice nodded, remembering what Mrs Hopkin had said about the queen's fifth child making it seem worse for her mistress.

'He hasn't come after her. Do you think he doesn't care for her?'

'Elizabeth has an idea he thinks his duty is to make money to keep her in comfort and that's what he's doing, hoping to get her back. Two more people not talking about the right things, Elizabeth says, when it would be so easy to understand one another.' Violet picked up the pile of mending, ready to take out to the laundry.

'So wise in some ways and so innocent in others.' She laughed. 'Elizabeth doesn't understand that saying what you feel to someone you love is sometimes the hardest thing in the world.'

She paused at the door.

'I've talked too much tonight. This is why I don't usually open my mouth. Please don't take any notice of me.'

'I won't tell anyone about any of it, I promise.'

In the end there was nothing to tell. Alice hadn't learned much at all, and nothing about Ivy and Daniel.

But she felt included and settled, though she knew it was only temporary.

'You'll come to church with us tomorrow?' Violet asked on the Saturday while they were all stopped for some food.

'Alice has been going to the one nearer the lodge,' Stanley said, looking at his mother.

'Is there another church? Where do you go?'

'We've always walked across the fields to St Luke's,' Stanley said. 'It was where my father used to go.'

'Funny how you get into the way of doing something and carry on even when it stops making sense,' Violet said.

'I'd never thought how much more convenient it would be to go to the other one.'

'It's our connection to him,' Stanley said. 'I just meant Alice may prefer to go to her usual place.'

'It is a connection,' Violet said, 'but we don't need it any more. He's in our hearts. We can go with Alice. I'd like for us all to be together for Easter.'

'No, please don't change your routine for me,' Alice begged. 'Especially at such an important time as Easter. If you don't mind, I'd love to come with you all to St Luke's.'

Stanley seemed pleased with the decision. Maybe he didn't want to see Ivy either.

She'd imagined Violet's family weren't churchgoers. Now the idea of being included with them on such a joyous occasion made her feel less lonely.

Unless Maggie was home for the day.

Unless Daniel was finished with his work or had come back for Easter.

'But I would like, if you'll allow me an

hour, to run to see Mr and Mrs Hopkin. They might wonder what's happened to me.'

'Someone will have told them.' Violet gave a little laugh as if admitting she was just as much a gossip as everyone else. 'Still, it's Easter Sunday. I'll walk down with you myself to say hello to Elizabeth.'

'Good,' Hetty put in. 'You need a holiday. We'll do whatever has to be done here.'

* * *

In the morning Alice found herself walking with Stanley, the rest of his family in front. The trail was well walked with other families around them on their way to celebrate the joy of the resurrection.

'Do you remember your father?' she asked.

'Barely. Do you have parents, Alice?'

Alice was surprised the news of her background hadn't reached him.

'No. I don't remember mine, either. But I had an aunt who took me in.'

'So no brothers or sisters, either?'

'No. You are fortunate with your family.' There was a silence. 'You work for Miss Little sometimes, don't you?'

He nodded.

'It helps to bring some money in, though I think sometimes I would help Miss Little for no payment.' He laughed. 'Don't let my mother hear me say so.'

'I know what you mean. She's been very good to me.'

'I think you've repaid her.'

What did that emphasis mean?

'You mean you feel you owe her something?'

'No, not me. You're a friend to Ivy as well, aren't you? I worry about Ivy.'

'Because of her mother?'

Stanley shook his head.

'Because of her father. She tells Miss Little her mother is ill and she has to take care of the children and then goes off with her father, she won't tell me where. I keep telling her it's wrong to misuse Miss Little so but she only laughs at me.'

'I worried too the last time I was there.

145

I feared she may lose her job. Her behaviour didn't seem quite . . . proper.'

'Miss Little makes a lot of allowances.'

'But Miss Little seems to be a person who sees more than other people. Do you think she's being taken in?'

'I think not.' Stanley looked at Alice. 'I think you may be someone else who sees things, Alice. What do you think of my mother?'

'I like her very much. I think she's someone who's had difficulties in life but not complained. She's worked hard and put her family first.'

'And yet yesterday she was worrying all day that she'd told you too much and you would think she was nothing but a gossip. May I tell her what you said?'

'Please do. I don't want her to worry. I admit I felt a little afraid of her when she came to the door for the laundry. She never stopped for a friendly word but I think she was always so pressed for time.

'I was surprised when she chatted so openly that first evening we sat sewing together. She was entertaining. We laughed but it was also clear she thought about things, about life.'

They were approaching what must be St Luke's. Stanley's brother lagged behind and fell into step beside them.

'There go the miller and his family,' he said. 'Go over to say hello and I will escort Alice into the pew.'

Alice looked over to where he was looking. The miller was a solid-looking man and his smiling wife had put flowers around her hat for Easter. There was someone who must be their daughter walking by her mother's side. The girl was pretty under her Easter bonnet and she looked up with a shy smile as she saw Stanley.

Ah, not Stanley and Ivy then. That was good. Ivy would be capable of hurting Stanley.

Daniel and Ivy, then? No, Alice did not want to believe that, not remembering the way Daniel had held her hands and how he had looked at her.

* * *

147

As they approached the farm that afternoon, Alice felt a tingle inside. Suppose Daniel were there?

There had been some discussion over whether Stanley would come with them.

'I don't think Daniel will be there,' he said. 'He was due to be away for a week or two.'

'Of course, you know Daniel from when you were children, don't you?' Alice longed to hear about their childhoods.

'He's only half a year older than me,' Stanley said. 'We spent a lot of time together as children. Before our parents set us to work.' He smiled at his mother. The affection between the two was clear.

'Come anyway to keep us company on the walk and say hello to Elizabeth and Graham,' Violet urged. 'Daniel may have managed to get home for Easter.'

Alice's heart leapt at that idea. Nice as it would have been to walk with Stanley, Alice was pleased he continued to turn down the invitation. She was determined the next time she saw Daniel to open her heart and to make sure he understood Charlie meant nothing to her. Indeed, that Charlie was now with someone else. She had Betty's letter saying so. It couldn't be plainer.

What would he tell her in return? Because he would open up to her as well, she knew it. Her reason told her it could be that he loved Ivy. Well, Alice would pick herself up and go on. Or Ivy loved him. That would be awkward but together they could overcome any difficulty.

Or, she supposed, Ivy was not involved at all but Daniel had no interest in Alice.

That, Alice's heart told her, was not possible. He'd touched her hand so tenderly, looked at her so lovingly. It was just a matter of — what was it Violet said Daniel's mother said? — talking about the right things.

Please let him be there, she thought now. On this hopeful day of resurrection, don't let her hopes be dashed.

Violet didn't converse much on the walk there and Alice nursed her hopes in silence.

The farmhouse was quiet, with no sign of anyone about.

'They'll be somewhere on the land, or feeding the hens,' Violet said. 'Like with laundry, there's always something that has to be done on a farm even of a Sunday.'

Alice laughed.

'It's a good thing we have Stanley feeding the mangle.' As soon as she said it she wondered at the 'we' and whether Violet would think her presumptuous. Tomorrow was sure to be her last day with them, after all. Or Tuesday, at best. There was no 'we'.

But Violet laughed as well and made her way out to the back, where Maggie's barn stood with the door closed and no figure hurrying out to greet them, straw in her hair.

Eventually, the person who appeared was Mr Hopkin.

'Ah, you are here,' Violet said happily.

'Only me, I'm afraid.' He greeted Violet in a friendly manner, then turned to Alice. 'Hello, Alice. Elizabeth will be sorry to miss you. She's taken the children to her brother's.'

'Her brother is back?' Alice's hopes soared again.

'No, and they are sorely missing him so they're cheering one another up.'

'I suppose Maggie didn't manage to get home today either.'

'That's the worst of it for Elizabeth, not knowing how young Maggie is faring. Come into the farmhouse,' he urged. 'There is cake left. Elizabeth won't forgive me if I don't pass on all your news, even if we have none of our own to give in return, and, Alice, I need to tell you about your robins. They're looking quite grown up.'

This wasn't what she'd hoped for but it was pleasant, very pleasant indeed. She was welcome and part of something very special. Surely this wouldn't be taken away from her, now she was starting to experience, albeit from the outside, the ordinary, loving family life she had longed for.

Secrets

Alice wondered whether they might see Ivy on the way back, or perhaps Miss Little out for a walk, but the long road up past 'their' church was strangely empty. Perhaps there had been an Easter parade that took everyone in a different direction, or they were all at home enjoying the chance to be with their families. She felt a strange contentment.

She'd been lifted out of her life and made her own way. It wasn't permanent or secure but she'd gained an understanding that she had the ability to change things. And that happiness was possible.

Of all the people she had considered they might see on the road — one more hoped-for than others — Stanley was not one of them. The sight of him clearly startled Violet as well because she hurried her pace.

'Stanley looks worried,' she said. 'I hope nothing's happened.'

'What is it?' she called when they were close enough for him to hear. 'Has there been an accident?'

'No, nothing like that,' he called. 'Don't fret, Ma.' But he wasn't smiling. 'Alice,' he said once he reached them, 'your Mrs Fleming has been.'

'Mrs Fleming!'

'Sir Edward sent a carriage for them. Their guests have left and he didn't want to pay another night in an inn when he has rooms in his own house.'

'Is that what he said to his own sister?' Violet asked. 'I knew he didn't care for her.'

'No, no, those are my words, Ma. Perhaps he can't wait to be close to her again.'

'Perhaps,' Violet said grimly. She didn't seem to believe it and Alice didn't, either.

'They wanted to take Alice with them,' Stanley went on.

'Don't tell me, they need her to help get the rooms ready.' Violet was clearly upset.

Alice was touched that Violet once again was on her side but her spirits drooped.

'We told her we'd take you there tomorrow, but she wasn't prepared to accept that,' Stanley said. 'She's not someone you can easily argue with, is she?' He looked upset.

'I thought she'd been brought low by what's happened this last week but she's evidently picked herself up and is back in charge. Are they waiting for me?'

'No. They made our Hetty pack your trunk and they took it. They're expecting you to follow as soon as you can. I'm sorry, Alice.'

'No, I'm sorry you had to do that for me.'

Stanley turned to walk back with them and it seemed to Alice they all slowed their pace.

'I could weep,' she said helplessly, hoping that would convey her appreciation to them both for having her to stay and everything they'd done.

Violet lifted her arms helplessly.

155

'I could weep for you.'

Just as Alice had convinced herself she was in control of her own life, this happened and showed her that no matter what dreams she had for herself she was really only an object in someone else's world and she was about to be picked up and placed somewhere else again.

★ ★ ★

'Mrs Fleming sent for me. I work for Lady Eleanor.'

The woman who had been called to see to Alice looked blank.

'We're very busy at the moment,' she said doubtfully. 'One set of guests has left and unexpected new guests might be arriving. It was a surprise and we're all of a muddle. I don't know where the housekeeper is. We haven't got time to deal with new staff as well today.'

'I think I'm supposed to be helping. I'm Alice.' The woman shook her head. 'Is Lady Eleanor here?'

'Could you come back tomorrow?'

156

'I was told to come straight away.' Alice wished she'd refused to do Mrs Fleming's bidding this time and stayed at Violet and Stanley's until morning. Now she could feel all the urgency of the downstairs of a big house with a lot going on and had no part in it.

And she couldn't go back to Violet's.

They'd all walked a short distance up the road with her.

'If I could afford to pay you a wage there would be a job for you with us,' Violet said.

'It would have to be a very good wage for Alice to afford her rent somewhere local,' Stanley said.

There. He'd been put out having to sleep next door. She'd earned her keep, all of them told her so, but it had clearly put them all out.

Then Stanley and his brother had accompanied her the rest of the way, as far as the gatehouse. What a kind family. She hadn't really looked at the front of the house or the drive leading up to it because of the tears in her eyes.

The brothers' kindness made her situation, as she was put into a room while the housekeeper was searched out, feel more wretched.

She hadn't necessarily expected to be welcomed with open arms but someone could at least have told them she was expected.

As the hustle and bustle abated, Alice could hear the sounds and smell the scents of the downstairs staff sitting down to supper. Her stomach rumbled. She wandered out to look for the person she'd spoken to, wondering if she had been forgotten.

There was no-one in sight and she didn't like to interrupt the meal, though she longed to be invited to eat with the others. Maggie would be there. She so wanted to speak to Maggie but more than anything she wanted to be included.

* * *

'Will you do me the honour of giving me your hand in marriage?' Alice was asking. 'Or do I need to ask your father first?'

Daniel shook his head and began to roar with laughter. His red hair started to change colour and he began to expand.

'My mother, you mean,' he said and as he got bigger and turned into Stanley Ivy appeared on his arm. And there was Daniel on her other arm.

'Wake up, Alice.'

It was all right, it was only a bad dream. She'd been asleep and now there was a familiar open face framed by reddish hair, looking at her with kind brown eyes.

'Daniel?' He'd come to help her, the way he had when she'd arrived at the lodge.

'Alice, it's me, Maggie. I've been sent to take you upstairs.'

Alice blinked.

'Maggie.'

'If I'd known you were here I'd have come to see you before.'

'Lady Eleanor sent for me — is she

here?'

'I don't know, nobody tells us what's going on but the housekeeper has been out all afternoon. She's only just found out you're here and I've offered to help find you somewhere to sleep.'

'My trunk is here somewhere.'

'Yes, one of the girls said there's a trunk been put in the room opposite her. I'll help you find it.'

Up the dark staircase to a corridor full of small rooms — it could have been Mr Younger's house, except it was bigger.

'Maggie, how are you faring here? Are you managing the work all right?'

'It's very confusing, Alice, but some of the girls are nice.' They reached an open door and Alice recognised her trunk on the floor. 'You're very tired,' Maggie said. 'We'll talk properly in the morning.'

Alice nodded. She was tired.

'Maggie,' a voice called, possibly the woman Alice had spoken to before. 'What are you doing there? That's not your part of the corridor at all.'

'I'm showing Alice her room. Alice has

come from Lady Eleanor's household and she's been left sitting downstairs for hours.'

Alice smiled. Maggie retained her spirit. She may have to warn her in the morning about talking back but her fears about Maggie being overwhelmed by life in the big house had not come to pass, at least not yet. She watched from the doorway as Maggie slipped into her own room. It was good to think that not far from her Maggie would be sleeping.

* * *

As she got dressed in the morning, Alice had the feeling she was the only one left up in the attic. She didn't know what time it was but all of the others must be at their work.

She tossed her head. Well, no-one had bothered to talk to her yesterday. She had been given no instructions to follow and as nobody had come to wake her today it looked as though she was going to be ignored again.

If she couldn't find Mrs Fleming today, she was ready to barge straight in to Sir Edward's best parlour to find out what was going on.

If Maggie could stand up for herself so could Alice. In the strange room in this strange house, after her experiences of the past weeks, Alice felt a settling. She wasn't a parcel to be picked up and put down and she wasn't a mouse afraid of what people would think if she spoke her mind.

She had gone where they sent her this time but she would make sure to get back and speak to Daniel. Life was too unpredictable to wait and hope. She lifted her head, took a deep breath and made her way downstairs.

The door to the room Alice had drowsed in the day before was open and someone was sitting behind the housekeeper's desk. Alice knocked and went in without waiting for a reply.

'I'm Alice,' she said. 'Lady Eleanor sent for me.'

'Alice, close the door, please.' The housekeeper was small and solid, with greying hair pulled back from a pale face. The high-necked dark dress drained the colour further from her.

When Alice had complied, the woman continued.

'I must ask you not to talk about Lady Eleanor in this house.'

Alice struggled to understand.

'Where is she?'

'You may stay here but on the condition you do not mention Lady Eleanor to anyone. Anyone. Do you understand?'

Well, of course she did, but Alice wanted to know why.

'Where is Mrs Fleming?'

'Or Mrs Fleming.' It looked as though the housekeeper didn't have much patience. 'Do you understand?'

'Yes, miss.' Alice realised that was as far as she could take the conversation. She lowered her eyes. 'How long am I to stay here?'

'I don't know.'

Alice felt as though the floor was

crumbling beneath her feet. She'd been dropped into a different life where there were no rules — except strange ones she had to obey without question and without understanding why.

Alice raised her eyes again to look at Sir Edward's housekeeper. She was older than Alice had first thought and there was a look of something like panic about her, as if she wasn't as in control of this situation as she wanted to pretend.

'I have a contract with . . . with my previous employers,' Alice told her. 'I'm paid quarterly and have Sunday afternoons off.'

'Very well, Sunday afternoon when it is convenient and I will have to discuss the arrangement for your wages. Find Gillian and see what jobs she has for you to do.'

'Thank you, miss.'

That would have to do for now. She wasn't confident Sunday was always going to be convenient but she would worry about that when the time came. She'd stated her case and that was a start.

'What's Sir Edward like to work for?' Alice asked the girls she was sent to work with. Gillian had turned out to be the woman who had spoken to her yesterday and she seemed to organise the female servants for the housekeeper.

'He's very fair,' the first one she asked said.

'They say he's a stickler,' a second, more talkative, one said.

'What, if we don't clean well enough?' Alice asked.

'No, he doesn't care about that so long as there's nothing visitors can criticise. In his business and properties, they say. And he worries what people think.'

'About the house?'

'And his family and the estate.'

'Does he have a wife and children?'

'Two children. He dotes on them.'

'So he's a decent person?'

'By all accounts, and fair to his staff. But however much of a stickler Sir Edward is, Mr Sim, the butler, is worse. You're best off keeping out of his way.'

Alice nodded. She was going to have

to dismiss any idea she may have been developing that Sir Edward had murdered his sister and her housekeeper and hidden their bodies although, as he was clearly someone who cared what people thought, there would be reason.

She'd run away from her husband and clearly that was something that left him open to gossip. How far would Sir Edward go to avoid that? She giggled to herself, sorry she wouldn't be able to discuss this story with Maggie.

As well as learning about the household, there were rules Alice would have to get used to. One morning she went down to get some soap and water.

'Alice, you shouldn't be down here while luncheon is being prepared for the family,' Gillian had told her.

'I thought they would be eating by now,' Alice said. She'd seen the footmen going up to the dining-room, surely? There were only Cook and Gillian in the kitchen. If luncheon was being prepared where were the other helpers? Where was the scullery maid who seemed to always be at the sink?

Gillian and Cook were preparing a tray of food. It looked as though someone was ill and was having luncheon in their room.

There was enough for two — maybe she had misunderstood what the footmen were doing and Sir Edward and his wife didn't have a formal meal in the dining-room at this hour. But from what she'd heard it didn't seem at all likely that Sir Edward would eat from a tray.

She waited quietly and when the tray was ready she saw Gillian take it out of the back door and round towards the front of the house.

'Are you ever allowed into the garden?' she asked the girl she was working with when she rejoined her.

'Sometimes,' the friendly girl said. 'Are you already feeling the need to escape? You've only been here a couple of days.'

Alice laughed.

'I like to know I can get out if I want to. I got used to hearing the birds sing at my last place.' As soon as the words were out Alice realised her mistake and hurried on, to avoid questions. 'Do Sir Edward and his wife ever eat in the garden?'

'I've never known it. He likes things just so.' The girl laughed. 'He wouldn't be at all pleased if a leaf blew into his soup.'

'Or a fly flew into his mouth.'

'It wouldn't dare.'

Alice remembered how much she liked sharing moments like this during the working day.

But there were secrets in this house and Alice couldn't help thinking they were tied up with Mrs Younger. Lady Eleanor.

The Library

'Sir Edward is expecting an important visitor and wants to show him his library.'

It was Thursday and Alice had not been able to find out where Mrs Younger and Mrs Fleming were. They weren't in the house, she was sure. All the talk was of meals for Sir Edward and his wife and for the children and no guests were mentioned.

Now the housekeeper was missing again and Gillian was handing out specific extra tasks as the servants finished their breakfast. Usually everyone kept their eyes down hoping not to be chosen but now Alice felt Maggie jump beside her and sit a little straighter.

'He wants all of the books taken out and dusted and the shelves cleaned. You need to have a good head for heights.' Gillian's eyes lit on Alice, who didn't avert her own eyes and who hadn't yet found her place in the household and so was useful for tasks like this.

Alice nodded.

'Maggie and I can do it, if we can be excused our other duties.'

Alice could feel Maggie's excitement beside her. She hoped she wasn't going to regret this. She could easily be left to do the hard work alone while Maggie looked at the books and they wouldn't get the job done in time.

But for now Gillian seemed grateful and Maggie could barely contain herself. Gillian took them upstairs and showed them the library.

Maggie was silent with awe but Alice thought the number of books overwhelming, ranged as they were on shelves on two sides of the room. Fortunately they did not go right up to the ceiling as a series of paintings lined up above the books, one close beside the other, all the same size, all as dark as one another, all of ships as far as Alice could make out. Even with the paintings, there must be hundreds of books.

'When is the visitor coming?' she asked.

'Saturday.' Gillian looked around and sighed. 'Just do your best in these two days.'

'We'll start at the top,' Alice said once Gillian had left. 'I'll hand the books down to you shelf by shelf. You must dust them and pile them up in order so we put them back in the right place. Maggie, are you listening? If we do this well it will be your job as long as you work here.'

She thought it would only be something Gillian would want the staff to do once a year but she had to entice Maggie with some reward for doing it properly.

Maggie nodded, her eyes shining.

'You dust them carefully and I'll wipe the shelf.'

Alice climbed the ladder gingerly. Given Maggie's agility in her barn it would have been easier to ask her to do this part of the job but Alice feared they wouldn't progress so quickly.

'This is heavy.' She passed the first one down to Maggie's outstretched hands. 'Don't drop it.'

Maggie took each one reverently and

lay it down with care. Alice shouldn't have had any fear that Maggie would not take care of the books.

'Can you tell whether they're in any order?' Alice asked after a while.

'These green ones are all the same,' Maggie said. 'They're about gardening, I think, or plants at least. They've all got different volume numbers. It'll be easy to get them back in order.'

'Not novels, then?' Alice smiled.

'I hope the novels are lower down.'

'Please don't hatch any plans to find out where they are and come in to read them another time.'

They laughed but the truth was that Alice was hatching plans of her own. It was too tempting not to go down to the kitchen again at the same time as yesterday to see whether two meals were being prepared and taken outside.

'Have you been into the garden, Maggie?'

'I've seen the vegetable garden. Pa wouldn't forgive me if I didn't explain to him what it is like.'

'Is there a summerhouse or a building out there?'

'Not that I've seen. There's a building a bit like your lodge in the grounds, quite near the entrance. Careful, Alice. You nearly dropped that one.'

'Sorry, Maggie. It's the last, anyway.'

And so the hours wore on until it was approaching the time Alice had spoken to Gillian the day before.

'That's another shelf done. You can start dusting all of those. I'll just wipe this shelf, then I need to . . . '

Alice couldn't think of an excuse to go below stairs after she'd been asked not to but she washed the bookshelf thoroughly and flew downstairs.

'Sorry, Gillian, I know you said not to come down for water but we're worried we're not putting the books back in the right place. Do you have some paper and a pencil so we can note the order down?'

Gillian looked doubtful.

Alice held her breath. A tray was being prepared in the kitchen.

'Don't take them all down at once,'

Gillian said vaguely.

'No, we're doing one shelf at a time.'

There was a sudden squeal from the kitchen.

'Ow.' It was Cook and it sounded as though she'd burned herself. 'My hand!'

'I've got to . . .' Gillian had a hand on the tray. 'But Cook needs to get her hand seen to.'

'Gillian!' Cook sounded in distress. 'Can't you come and help me, please?'

'I can take that,' Alice said. 'Where does it have to go?'

'Gillian, hurry!'

Alice picked the tray up.

'Out of here.' Gillian pointed to the kitchen door. 'Turn right, then left. Give it to the person outside the house there.'

Alice nodded and went towards the doors. 'And, Alice — not a word to anyone, all right? No-one.'

'Yes, Gillian.'

It was a small brick-built structure. In shape it was in the style of the lodge, it was true, but half the size. Alice made her way round to the front and there stood a short, solid young man barring the way.

'I'll take that,' he said.

'Gillian said I have to take it in.' Alice didn't look him in the eye but held on to the tray and eventually he yielded and stood aside.

'Hello?' Alice called as she went in. She hoped she was right about who she was going to find here and she wouldn't be confronted by a stranger.

'Alice, thank goodness.'

Alice beamed. So Mrs Fleming had been worried about her and was relieved she was safe.

Mrs Fleming came out of what must be the front parlour and closed the door behind her.

'What's happening?' Alice asked.

Mrs Fleming lowered her voice.

'Sir Edward is keeping his sister here hoping she'll come to her senses, as he says, and go back to her husband. She won't do that and says her husband has to come to her of his own accord. You must get a message to Mr Younger to tell him she's being held against her will and needs to know he cares for her.'

'Mrs Fleming, I can't do that.'

'You must. Mrs Younger is barely eating and is ill. But you mustn't breathe a word of any of this to anyone.'

'How can I do this? And how can I do it without asking for help?' Mrs Fleming clearly didn't remember what life was like for a servant. She couldn't get in a carriage and go to Mr Younger's house even if she thought he would speak to her when she arrived. Alice thought quickly. 'If I could get to Miss Little's she could send a letter.'

'Yes, do so, Alice. I'm counting on you. But tell no-one but Miss Little.'

Alice hesitated.

'I haven't been paid since Christmas. Could you give me the money to give to Miss Little for a stamp or a messenger?'

Mrs Fleming went quickly upstairs and came back with something in her hand.

There was a sound at the door.

'Take this,' Mrs Fleming said.

As Alice made her way back to the

house she wondered at the speed with which life presented her with new problems. Now she had to make sure she was given Sunday off to get to Miss Little's. And not tell anyone else why she had to see her so urgently.

She also realised Mrs Fleming's 'Thank goodness' hadn't been relief about her own welfare at all. It was because she was supposed to rescue them.

'Alice, where have you been?'

When she returned to the library, Alice realised she had no paper and pencil to explain her disappearance.

'Oh, I just went down to . . . There was an accident in the kitchen. Cook burned her hand.'

'Is she all right?'

Alice had no idea. She'd been so agitated when she flew back into the house she hadn't noticed or spoken to anyone. Poor Cook. She should at least have enquired.

'I think so. I see you've continued. Well done, Maggie.'

'There's one poor book that's badly

broken. I've left it on the desk so some-one can tell Sir Edward. I've left a space where it goes.' Maggie took a book from the pile on the floor and carried it up the ladder. 'Can you pass me the next one up?' She nodded towards the one on the table. 'It wouldn't do for Sir Edward's visitor to get that one out and it falls apart as soon as he opens it.'

Alice was glad Maggie was talking and that she had this job under control. Her own heart was still thumping.

She had so many secrets to keep and now a shilling in her pocket that she thought the whole world would be able to see.

'I wonder if there is such a job as a mender of books,' Maggie went on. 'That would be the best job in the whole world.'

As they worked on Alice lost all sense of time. She couldn't remember what day it was and worried how she could ensure she got to Miss Little's on Sunday. She had no doubts that Miss Little would help her.

'I hope it's not the last time I do something for you,' she'd said the day Alice went to Violet's. Was that really only a week ago?

She wondered how time was passing for Mrs Younger and Mrs Fleming. Mrs Younger never seemed to do anything much since she'd left her husband's house but Mrs Fleming was always busy. Keeping the mistress's spirits up must be a thankless task, and to be stuck in that house unable to leave. Alice shuddered and then laughed as her stomach rumbled loudly in the quiet room.

'When we've finished this shelf, shall I run down to see how close it is to supper time, or whether they've forgotten us?'

'Yes, do, Maggie.'

After Maggie left, Alice dusted her hands on her apron and went over to the desk. Maggie had left the book open, the missing pages carefully laid in the right place. It would be skilled work repairing this. There was no way an ordinary person could get the pages far enough into the spine so they sat evenly with the others.

She turned to mention this to Maggie as she heard the door open. If only Maggie could be trained to do this, surely she would be the happiest worker alive. But it wasn't Maggie. A man in a black suit with a waistcoat came in, looking haughtily at Alice.

He was too old to be Sir Edward. This must be Mr Sim, the butler. He spotted the book on the desk and hurried over.

'What have you done here, girl?'

Alice almost felt she should curtsey as she answered, so far above her did this man seem.

'We didn't know whether Sir Edward was aware this one is broken, sir,' she said. 'We've left it out to make sure he knows.'

Mr Sim gave her a withering look. It made Alice feel guilty even though she had done nothing wrong. Her hand crept unbidden under her apron to her pocket.

'You're a pert creature,' he said. 'What have you got there in your pocket?'

Once again Alice had that feeling of the floor opening out underneath her.

'It's something someone gave me, sir. May I go to supper now?'

The butler looked as though he was going to explode. Now she'd said the wrong thing.

'When I've seen what you're hiding.'

'I need to speak to Gillian.'

'Gillian can't protect you if you've been stealing. Empty your pocket, girl.'

The coin sat on the desk with the book, two pieces of evidence for the haughty Mr Sim, who wasn't interested in truth.

Not that she could tell him.

'You'll leave in the morning.'

'We didn't damage the book. It was already like that. And the coin was given to me.'

'By who?'

'I need to speak to Gillian.'

'You will leave in the morning.'

Gillian wouldn't help her either. She'd gone against Gillian's wishes by taking the tray into the house and talking to Mrs Fleming. Talking to someone she wasn't allowed to mention. Someone who was counting on her to rescue their mistress. Which she now had to achieve with no money.

At least he hadn't thrown her out in the dark and at least she could have supper tonight.

Except now she was going to have to sit at the table knowing it was her last meal here and not being able to tell anyone, even Maggie.

How had she managed to get herself into this situation while trying only to do good?

Talking It Over

Alice was up and out before anyone else the next morning, having barely slept for thinking her situation round in circles. One thought that kept returning was that she could stay and speak privately to the housekeeper and Gillian, whose secrets she was keeping.

There was, though, a chance they would sacrifice her for the good name of their master. A good chance. She had, after all, gone out of her way to speak to Mrs Fleming after they specifically told her she was not to be so much as mentioned.

And if she stayed, somebody, Mr Sim himself perhaps, could find a way to prevent her going out on Sunday. The probability was there was a church nearby and she would have to go to that one and that would count as Alice's day off.

Then there was the question of Maggie. If Mr Sim forced any further discussion about the book, Maggie might be in difficulties too. Alice had never known a butler get involved in matters to do with the female staff but this one had and he seemed capable of bearing a grudge.

In Mr Younger's house Mrs Fleming dealt with the maids and talked to the butler every day. They respected one another and wouldn't interfere in the other's realm.

If Sir Edward's housekeeper was never there, which she seemed not to be, you couldn't blame Mr Sim for being tempted to get involved, although in this case his action had been very wrong.

Alice knew that in some houses the mistress would place coins in unexpected places to see if anyone who found it while they were cleaning would keep it or not. The maids couldn't win because if they didn't find it, or if they left it there, they'd be accused of not cleaning properly.

Perhaps that was what they did here and Mr Sim had assumed she'd kept a shilling she'd found on the bookshelf.

Alice's next thought was that if she managed to see Miss Little today that task would be done and it would be out of her hands, and Mrs Fleming would be freed sooner.

Imagine not being able to open the door and step out, even to hear the bird-song.

So Alice had packed her trunk again and left the room neat. If only she could write a note to Maggie to explain.

As she left the house and breathed the sweet morning air, Alice had an idea she might just be able to open the door and let Mrs Younger and Mrs Fleming out. But the same man who had barred her way the day before was sitting propped against the door, fast asleep.

Alice laughed to herself as she strode along. Could Mrs Younger even have walked the five or six miles to Miss Little's? Then she felt bad for laughing. Suppose her mistress really was ill?

Alice slowed her pace as she left the house behind. She didn't want to arrive too early.

She hoped Ivy wouldn't be there.

Alice had an idea she would wait near the lodge until people were up and about. She'd have to make sure Sir Edward's agent wasn't there but that could be easily assessed, and the back door may well not be open.

She could check on her robins, at least. If she got in, she could make tea. That would be welcome. It would be like coming home to her own cottage.

If only Daniel would be waiting for her. She couldn't even decide what to do after she'd seen Miss Little — all her focus was on getting that done first. She couldn't work out her next step.

Well, she had all day to think about where she would sleep. She couldn't ask Violet, that was for sure, and the Hopkins didn't have any spare space either.

Maggie's barn! She would ask if she could sleep in Maggie's barn for a couple of nights.

And probably she should ask Miss Little to ask Mr Younger to take her back. Betty had thought she would be welcome.

Despite the incident with Mr Sim, all of Alice's being cried out that given the choice she would stay at Sir Edward's rather than return to Mr Younger's.

It would be awkward with Charlie and she had been replaced. But that wasn't all, not even the main reason.

It was too far from Daniel.

Alice dawdled so much the main street was beginning to be busy when she reached it but Miss Little's house was quiet, the curtains drawn.

She wondered what time the cook arrived, what time Ivy started. She loitered by the door for a moment and a neighbour came out, looking at her suspiciously.

'I don't want to disturb Miss Little too early,' Alice explained.

'Oh, you're the girl who helped out last week, aren't you? Miss Little isn't there.' The neighbour shook her head. 'She's away at her sister's.'

'Do you know how long for?' Miss Little wouldn't have started Alice doing the paperwork, wouldn't have begun teaching her to read, if she was planning to go away on a long trip.

'She didn't know. Her sister twisted an ankle and can't walk far. She didn't know how long she would need help for. I'm sure Miss Little would have told you herself but she organised it in a hurry.'

'Does the sister live near?'

'No, it's more than half a day's journey, she always says. She's a brave woman, is Miss Little.'

'Thank you.' Alice surprised herself that she remembered her manners when now the ground really opened up beneath her.

All her hopes had been placed on the certainty that Miss Little would help her. And now Miss Little was gone.

There was a buzz in Alice's head and her chest felt so tight she couldn't breathe. She ran down to the place where you would turn off to get to the lodge. A horse and cart with two men in it was coming along from the direction she'd come, but there was time to cross before it was near her.

Alice ran over the road and up the path towards the lodge. It seemed to her the cart stopped and she looked over her shoulder as she reached the corner of the lodge to see a shape following her.

Alice felt sick.

If she turned suddenly and ran she could surprise the man, dash past him and be out on the road before he could touch her. If she called out to Miss Little's neighbour or made a fuss in the street he might give up and let her go.

She glanced behind. He was running towards her and calling her name. The light falling on his red hair made him look like an angel. Only one man would look so.

'Daniel!'

Alice turned and he folded her in an embrace. He pulled back a little to look at her with such tenderness Alice felt she could no longer contain all the emotion she held. She reached up to kiss him and his lips were soft and warm on hers.

It was not like kissing Charlie, where

she didn't know quite what to do and found she was just waiting for it to be over.

She hadn't known it but this was what she'd dreamed of all these years.

'Have you finished your work, Daniel? You're home to stay?' Alice led the way up the path, now getting overgrown again. She reflected that you tread your path once but can't sit back, you have to keep tending it.

'Yes. We have some more orders over that way and will have to go back but the repairs are finished for now.'

'That's good, isn't it, that there is more work?' She tried the handle of the back door.

The door opened.

'We're not living here any more.' Alice looked in the provisions to see if there was still tea and went to the tap to fill the kettle, then realised there was no point lighting the fire for one lot of water.

Unless she moved back in for a few days while she worked out what to do.

'What happened to you?' Daniel asked.

Alice left the idea of tea.

'I'm holding secrets for people,' she said.

He nodded.

'Tell me what you can,' he said. 'If they are people who merit your loyalty I won't ask you to break their trust.'

'I hadn't thought whether they merit my loyalty. It was my own promise I thought of.'

'Alice, you're trembling. Are you unwell?'

'I would like to sit down.' Alice thought about the fix she was in. 'Daniel, I would like to sit in the parlour. I want to know what it's like to sit in a parlour and converse. It's a long story, Daniel, about how it's been for me this last week, but if you'll listen I'm going to tell you everything.'

'Do tell me.' He sat beside her and took her hand and squeezed it every now and then as she spoke.

'I don't always make the right decisions, Daniel,' she told him when she was finished. She didn't feel like a heroine in this story. Maggie would have made it different. 'Do you think I was wrong not to fight for my place?'

He shrugged.

'You couldn't know how that would turn out either. You were concerned to carry out Mrs Fleming's instructions — and to protect my sister.' He reached across and took Alice's other hand and something deep inside her tingled.

'I was on my way home with my uncle when I saw you, Alice, and I begged him to let me out. My mother doesn't know I'm back. I should go to her and you must come, too.'

Alice nodded. She was too exhausted to argue.

'I wondered if I could beg to sleep tonight in Maggie's barn. I don't know what to do. I'm so tired, Daniel.'

He stood up and tugged Alice up with him, then gently wrapped his arms around her.

'I don't think my mother would have you sleep in a barn, my love. Me and my brothers, perhaps.'

'No, that can't happen,' Alice began,

remembering Stanley. Then she stopped and realised what he had said.

My love.

She searched for his lips again and found she had some strength after all.

She thought she had strength enough to kiss and be kissed by Daniel Hopkin for all eternity.

★ ★ ★

As they got closer to the house, Alice could see Daniel peering beyond the building and thought he was looking to see if he could spot where his father was working.

'Have you missed your family?'

'It's interesting to see further afield,' Daniel said. 'But I always like to come home. I'm happy to know Maggie is faring well away.' He glanced at Alice. 'Though she'll be sad about what happened to you.'

'I pray she has the sense to keep quiet about her part in the broken book — though her only part was finding it and caring enough to want Sir Edward to know about it.'

'And get it mended, I expect. She wouldn't like any pages to get lost.'

'From what I heard, Sir Edward likes things to be just so. Maggie wanted to save him the embarrassment of it seeming to fall apart in his guest's hands.' She smiled. 'She should be thanked for considering his feelings.'

'I wonder if he knows his butler behaves so.'

'He'll just be concerned that everything runs smoothly upstairs. Thinking about Sir Edward's household makes me a little more grateful to Mrs Flem . . .'

Daniel interrupted before she could finish.

'No. She's the one who has caused your dilemma. She thinks only of herself.'

'About her mistress, perhaps.' Then Alice laughed. 'I'm sad about the shilling, though. I've never had anything that anyone has stolen before.'

'It was criminal of him to take it.'

A man was coming towards them on the path who Alice recognised. A small, grey-faced man. She faltered and stepped behind Daniel to move to the other side of him, away from the person approaching.

The two men nodded at one another and passed without a word and apparently with little warmth between them.

'Who is that man?' she asked.

'He's Ivy's father. Do you know him?'

'The week before you went away he came to the kitchen door of the lodge, pretending to be a traveller. I gave him food and water but asked him to go when I felt he was too interested in looking about him. I followed him out and he was with another man who I didn't see, talking about the inside of the house.

'It was a few days later — the day you and Maggie both left — that someone broke in. Nothing was taken but it caused Mrs Fleming to feel unsafe. I think she may have sent for Sir Edward.'

'You think it could have been him who broke into the lodge?'

'I did think so but perhaps I was wrong to. I didn't know he was Ivy's father.'

Daniel sighed.

'No. You're right to be suspicious. He doesn't have a good reputation.'

'Why would he be visiting here?'

'I think my mother gives him food sometimes but he doesn't seem to be carrying anything today.'

'Might she have refused him? I would be surprised.'

'Sometimes she thinks the food doesn't go into the mouths of his children.'

'Do you think he's been in prison? People talk of him going away and stop themselves actually saying where.'

'He has, Alice. It was hard for Ivy and people wanted to protect her from the scandal. Now, I'm sorry if you are fond of Ivy but she is becoming more like him.'

'I do recall the Sunday before her father came to the door she was interested in seeing where I lived. She wanted to go inside but Mrs Fleming was there. I hope she wasn't looking so that she could report back to her father.'

They walked in silence for another minute. Alice shivered. Suppose Ivy had been using her to help her father steal from the lodge? Was Alice such an innocent that she'd been thinking of friendship and that was the real aim of the possible friend?

She was pleased to reach the warm comfort of the Hopkins' farmhouse and be offered fresh bread and jam that already smelled of summer.

She listened to Daniel tell about his work and the time with his uncle while she enjoyed her meal. All the time her mind was examining her own dilemma but she was jolted from her thoughts by Daniel's next question.

'What was Ivy's father doing here?' he asked his mother. 'We saw him leaving.'

'He wanted to see you, Daniel. It's late in the day for him to show concern but Ivy is set on a course of action he can't talk her out of. He wanted you to try.'

'He thought I would be able to convince her? I wonder he didn't stop to ask in the road.'

'Perhaps he would have if you had been alone. He remembers Ivy once listened to you.'

'Did she? When we were five years old, perhaps. It's the man he brought into their lives who holds sway over her now.'

'And over him. I've never seen him so worried.'

'But you sent him away.'

'I said if we can prevent Ivy taking part in a robbery we will but that he should have considered her much sooner.'

'I don't know anyone Ivy would listen to,' Daniel said.

'Stanley talked about wanting to help her and that she wouldn't listen to him either,' Alice put in. 'And she disrespects Miss Little so.'

Mrs Hopkin nodded.

'If her father cannot scare her with stories of prison then I don't know how else to stop her. The man he met there has Ivy enraptured.'

'He's the sweetheart she speaks of?'

Daniel laughed.

'Ivy always speaks of having a sweetheart. For a time she claimed it was me and I had to put up with the villagers teasing me about it. Maggie has never forgiven her for inventing such a story and making our family the subject of gossip.'

Alice expelled a breath silently. So much worrying and it was so simple?

'Well, that's all over now, thank goodness.' Mrs Hopkin spoke briskly. 'Now, Alice, if you have eaten enough tell me what has happened to you since you were here with Violet on Easter Day.'

'That same day I went up to Sir Edward's house and I spent some time with Maggie. She is doing well there. I left in a hurry but am sure if she could have given me messages for you all I would have brought affectionate greetings.'

'I wonder why she hasn't written.'

'I expect the rules of the house are confusing and she needs to find her way with what is allowed. She takes it all seriously and is working hard. They should be pleased with her.'

'That is good. May I ask why you left? Are Mrs Younger and Mrs Fleming back here too?'

'I believe Mrs Younger is being held against her will in a building on the estate, and Mrs Fleming too. I think Sir Edward is trying to convince her to go back to her husband. That's why I'm here. I need to find a way of telling Mr Younger.'

There was a long silence.

'I hoped Miss Little would be able to help me,' Alice said in a small voice.

Then she shook her head. She wasn't going to admit she'd had an idea of hiring a carriage and going to Mr Younger's house.

She didn't know if her shilling would have been enough to do that but Miss Little would have known how to find out. Or would certainly have written a letter.

While they'd been talking about other things, Alice's mind had been busy.

'I'm going to see the rector,' she announced. 'He wasn't kind to Mrs

Younger but he ought to agree to help me free her. And Mr Younger might listen to him.'

'Maybe.'

Alice saw Daniel exchange a glance with his mother. It looked as though they didn't think it was a good idea.

'If that doesn't work perhaps I can find someone else to write a letter for me to the butler at Mr Younger's house. He's a decent person, I think, and has the ear of his master. And I think he respects Mrs Fleming and will want to help her.' She stopped to think. 'It's a lot to ask someone but perhaps Maggie . . . '

She was pleased to see Mrs Hopkin smile, and exchange a different sort of glance with her son.

'Of all of my children,' she said, 'I would say Daniel has the best hand.'

At the Hopkins'

Alice stood up and paced to the door and back. 'I don't like having to ask people to do things for me.'

Daniel looked up at her as she came to stand in front of him.

'And yet you readily agreed to help Violet, and Miss Little, and my mother over Maggie, and you collected the eggs for us without question the Sunday you were here. And you lost your job in order to try to help Mrs Fleming.'

Alice sat down as something shifted in her world.

'You must not weigh the kindness and favours you do so lightly you can't accept kindness and favours from others,' Daniel added.

She nodded.

'Besides,' Daniel went on, 'my mother will probably ask you to stir the cheese this afternoon. Will you refuse?' He laughed.

'No, you'll offer before she asks and

do it willingly. Now, what is the name of the butler at Mr Younger's house?'

'Dear Mr Mason

I was in service in Mr Younger's household for five years before Mrs Fleming asked me to accompany her and Mrs Younger on their present visit.

I have now found out that my mistress is being held against her will in a house on the estate of her brother, who I only know as Sir Edward. Sir Edward is not a bad man but apparently wants to force her to return to her husband, which she will not do until she is assured of his affection. On this she is most insistent.

Mrs Fleming is being held in the house as well and is most anxious about the health of the mistress.

I believe you held Mrs Fleming in high esteem.

Are you able to bring this situation to the attention of Mr Younger and urge him to act?'

Alice nodded as Daniel read the

letter through to her. It would have to do. Different words wouldn't make a difference if Mr Mason was unwilling to take notice of a housemaid or Mr Younger of his butler.

'Do you know how to get it into the post?'

Daniel grinned.

'I have to go to my uncle's. I'll do it on the way.'

'Thank you.' She smiled, feeling lighter. 'Now, I have to see if there is butter to churn or cheese to stir.'

* * *

'Is your arm aching, Alice?'

'You would think this was the sort of action you could do without thinking but you have to concentrate to keep the same rhythm.'

'When you've done it for as many years as I have it becomes easier and the butter tells you when it's done.'

'It does feel different now to when I started. Could it be ready?'

'Not yet.' Mrs Hopkin opened the churn and Alice could see the milk was no longer liquid but was definitely not butter.

Alice laughed.

'No. That looks more like cream. Close it up and I'll keep churning.'

'You're right you need to concentrate. Maggie forgets and starts to turn more slowly or more quickly, depending what part the story in her head is at.'

'I hope Maggie is well.'

'She'll be wondering where you went.'

'I fear she will. There are a lot of secrets in that house.' Alice stopped herself from expressing the hope that Maggie was not getting herself into trouble by asking questions. There was no point in worrying her mother even more.

'Mrs Hopkin, I was wondering if you or Mr Hopkin might object if I slept in your barn for a few nights. I mean where Maggie does her reading,' she added quickly, 'not the barn you use.

'Or did I misunderstand and you use that one as well? It would be just until I work out what to do.'

'I was thinking about putting you in with the two younger girls but if Maggie manages to get home and stay overnight it would be a squeeze.'

'Yes, Daniel mentioned that too but I worry the inconvenience would be too much for everyone. Poor Stanley had to sleep at his brother's while I was there and he was pleased when I left.'

'I'm sure he didn't say that.'

Alice laughed.

'No, he said he didn't want me back there in a hurry.'

'Alice, I'm sure Stanley would say no such thing.' Now Mrs Hopkin was laughing, too.

There was a noise outside.

'There's Graham,' Mrs Hopkin said. 'I'll just . . .'

So she needed to warn him. Alice knew it was wrong to leave the churn and wrong to eavesdrop on a private conversation but she crept to the door anyway.

'Alice is here,' Mrs Hopkin was saying.

'Oh. Didn't she go up to the big house

after all?'

'Yes. Violet's boys walked her up there on Sunday. But something happened — I'm not quite clear what. To do with damage to something they were cleaning and Alice made sure Maggie didn't get into trouble, but she got thrown out herself.'

No. That wasn't right. Maggie was never in danger of being dismissed — was she?

'That sounds like Alice,' Mr Hopkin said.

'She can tell us the whole story over supper,' Mrs Hopkin said. 'Lady Eleanor is being imprisoned there.'

'Surely not.'

'She'll explain it all.'

She will, Alice determined. She was not going to be made the heroine of a story where her role had been less active.

'For now, we're discussing sleeping arrangements,' Mrs Hopkin told her husband. 'Could the boys sleep in the barn for a few nights?'

'No need. We'll have the girls in with

us.'

'Are you sure?' Mrs Hopkin sounded doubtful. 'They're bigger than they used to be.'

Mr Hopkin laughed.

'Well, I'm smaller than I used to be. It's not possible that Daniel has become so tall.'

Alice dashed back to the churn. There was a tear in her eye and this time it wasn't of despair or rage.

* * *

Alice was cleaning the kitchen the next morning while everyone else was about farm chores.

A soft voice she knew called a 'Hello' from the open door and there stood Stanley with a parcel of the kind she recognised. So Mrs Hopkin used her friend Violet's services as well.

'I didn't expect to see you here,' Stanley said. 'Have they given you a day off so soon?'

Alice laughed.

'It's a long story, Stanley, and I'll always be grateful for your kindness and your brother's for getting me there safely, but I lasted only four days and they dismissed me.'

Stanley opened his mouth but apparently couldn't speak for a moment.

'Why?' was all he said eventually.

'A misunderstanding. I think we'll sort it out but for now here you find me. Let me take the laundry from you. Mrs Hopkin is about somewhere but, tell me, does she usually sit you down with a drink and a bite or are you too pressed?'

Stanley smiled.

'It's usually my mother who does the collection and delivery and I believe they do allow themselves a moment to catch up when they both can, but despite your help last week we're behind again with the mending so my mother asked me to come today.'

'I must see if I can come along to help for a few hours,' Alice said. 'I must use my time between places wisely.'

'Yes, and my mother would never

forgive me if she thought I'd as good as asked you to come and do her sewing again.'

'But she can't stop me offering.'

'I had hoped to see Daniel — is he about?'

'I believe he's working with his uncle.'

'You'll be interested, too, Alice, and maybe you can tell him. Ivy told me as bold as brass that the man she is associating with is planning a robbery and she's going to help him.'

'Why would she tell you?'

'She likes to tease me for not being as bold as she is. It was as though she was daring me to go to the constable.'

'Will you?'

'She knows I will not. We agreed when we were children, the three of us, to look out for one another.'

'Could it be that she has got herself further into a bad situation and is hoping you'll get her out of it?'

Stanley looked doubtful.

'That's possible, I suppose.'

'Did she tell you when and where?'

'I didn't know how to take the hints she gave me, about the lodge and Miss Little's house.'

'There's nothing in the lodge. And that she would treat Miss Little so is shocking.'

'There will be furniture and plate in the lodge that will be saleable. But I'm most worried about Miss Little.'

'How could she do that to someone who has been kind to her?'

'She seems to have little heart these days. She admitted to me they once put her through a window and she opened the front door for them to walk into someone's house. She wasn't even ashamed, Alice.'

'They? Is it the man she calls her sweetheart we are talking about?'

'He and her father. They met in prison, by all accounts.' He sighed. 'Ivy was so brave when it first happened, Alice. She wouldn't let people talk ill of her mother. We thought they would not allow the father back but they did and now it's been more than once. She's lost that spirit that allowed her to stand up to him and to people who talked about him.'

'It sounds as though she's become more like him instead. How can we stop her? Do we know when all this is planned for?'

'I told her she could not be sure Miss Little would be away for much longer and that Lady Eleanor could be back any day. It wasn't lying. Nobody knows and these things are possible. I meant to say it was too risky for her to do at all but she took it that they would need to hurry and do it today.'

'Do you think Daniel will be able to stop her?'

Stanley shook his head.

'No. Not really.' He smiled and lifted his hands helplessly. 'Ivy always took risks. When we were children between us Daniel and I could usually talk her out of doing anything too dangerous she had in mind to do but she's changed.'

'I'll tell him and if he sees her he can try to speak to her. That will be something. If she really wants to be saved that might do it.'

As Stanley left, Mrs Hopkin came in with a basket of vegetables.

'This is for delivery but I have to look at the butter. If it is well drained I can pat it into shape and add some to the basket.'

'And I'll deliver it for you so you may get on with your other tasks.' Alice smiled happily. 'Unless you were looking forward to getting out.'

'We'll go to church together tomorrow, shall we? I'll feel freer to dawdle then with all the chores done. And you may want to check on your robins on the way back today.'

The butter was soon patted into a block, and from the directions Alice realised she was headed for the house of the neighbour of Miss Little she had spoken to the day before. The woman was expecting visitors, she'd told Mrs Hopkin, and had requested an extra delivery.

This was why she'd mentioned the robins — Alice would have to go twice past the lodge. It was a way of giving permission to Alice to linger.

As she left the busy neighbour preparing for her visitors, Alice looked warily at Miss Little's house. The windows were intact, curtains drawn and the door firmly closed. It would be hard for anyone to break in here without the neighbours seeing and she couldn't have asked about the way in the back without alarming the neighbour.

Instead she walked to the end of the row of cottages and turned left along the side of the last one, then left again.

'What are you doing here?'

Ivy's blonde hair was piled on to the back of her head and she wore a dull brown dress. She had no smile for Alice.

'What are you doing here?' Alice replied, as Ivy came close, took her arm and turned her around.

Alice peered back the way Ivy had come. It seemed to her that a man dodged back behind a wall but Alice didn't know if she was seeing what she expected to see.

'Miss Little isn't home, is she?' Alice asked, as Ivy wasn't answering her question.

'No. I keep an eye on her house while she's away. There are people up to no good everywhere. Why are you nosing around?'

'Like you, I was worried about the safety of Miss Little's cottage. I didn't know whether there was a way in at the back or not.'

'Why are you here anyway? Didn't you get another position? Miss Little got the wrong idea about who you are but you're only a maidservant, aren't you?'

A sly smile came over Ivy's face as Alice struggled for an answer. There was no pretence at friendship here.

'You didn't get the position, did you? You weren't good enough for Sir Edward.'

They both looked up at the sound of a carriage and Alice felt her heart begin to beat irregularly and her stomach clenched. Surely that was Mr Younger's carriage, stopping at the end of the road leading up to the lodge.

The footman had got down and was engaging a passer-by in conversation. Ah, they were asking for directions. Was it possible Mr Younger didn't know where his wife's brother lived now? At least it was the pleasant footman she'd met before. Alice tore herself from Ivy's grip and ran forward.

'Frederic. I'm Alice,' she added in case he couldn't place her out of her uniform and with her hair hanging free. 'Are you looking for Sir Edward's house?'

'Yes. Hello, Alice. The coachman thought it would be past the lodge house but can't see how to get there but this man says Sir Edward lives somewhere else now.' He lifted a hand to the stranger. 'Thank you,' he called then turned back to Alice. 'You know where it is, do you?'

'I can climb up with the coachman and show him.' Alice surprised herself with her confident suggestion. She looked doubtfully up to the coachman's seat and laughed. 'How do I get up there? Do I have to step on the wheel?'

From the corner of her eye Alice saw Ivy still standing where she had left her, openly staring. Perhaps, like Alice herself, she was comparing her to the mouse who had come to the village less than two months before.

She couldn't think what had happened to that fearful Alice who barely had the faith in herself to tackle the things she knew she could do, much less look up to the height of the seat in this carriage and imagine herself up there. She who had been so fearful being inside this same carriage.

'Is this the girl who wrote?' came a voice from the window.

'Yes, Mr Younger. I'm Alice, one of your housemaids.'

'Tell the footman where to go and get in.'

She gave Frederic the directions and approached the side of the carriage. This time she had the sense to realise there was a step up. Then Frederic closed the door and she was inside, facing Mr Younger, realising she didn't even know whether he was still her employer or not.

Mrs Fleming Back in Charge

'I'm sorry I wasn't clearer in my letter,' Alice said as Mr Younger continued to look at her. He probably didn't know how to talk to her any more than she did to him.

'We haven't been to visit since they moved.'

Alice nodded. She could imagine Sir Edward might not make his title-less brother-in-law welcome but for form's sake you would have thought he'd maintain contact. The man in the carriage seemed quite inoffensive. She tried to remember whether Sir Edward and his family had visited Mr Younger's house but saw from the corner of her eye Daniel with his uncle in their horse and cart.

What was she thinking? She had to make sure Mrs Hopkin wasn't going to worry about her.

'Excuse me, Mr Younger. May I let my friends know where I am going?'

She put a hand out to open the door and jump out as Mr Younger called to the coachman to stop.

The footman was down in a trice to open the door.

Fortunately, Daniel's uncle had been slowing his own horse as they approached the carriage and Daniel got down as quickly as Alice did.

'Is that Mr Younger's carriage?' Daniel was beaming. 'It worked?'

Alice grinned as well.

'I was out doing a delivery for your mother and the coachman wasn't certain where to go so I'm showing them. Will you tell your mother? She may worry if I'm gone long.

'Oh, and Daniel, Ivy's planning a robbery with that man she knows who's got the ugly voice and Stanley wants you to help talk her out of it. She's just down there, near Miss Little's. Stanley thinks it's Miss Little's house they're planning to enter and the lodge as well.'

'Yes, yes, but, Alice, if they make you stay, get word to us,' Daniel said urgently.

'They won't make me do anything. I'm someone who knows how to get in and out of carriages now.' Alice laughed. She felt giddy at the idea as she turned ready to run back to Mr Younger.

Then another thought struck her. She was about to try to convince Mr Younger he had to tell his wife he loved her.

They could make her stay. She may be drunk on her own importance now but she still needed work. If she could urge Mr Younger to have the right conversation she had to be able to do it herself.

'Daniel, you're right. I'll have to do what they say. Remember I love you.'

He looked shocked then took her in his arms for a moment that was all too brief and she hugged him tight.

'And I love you.' He stood looking at her as she tore herself away. 'If you can't come back or get a message to us I'll come and look for you.'

She nodded and ran.

Daniel and his family couldn't take care of her indefinitely, there was no place at Violet's for long. She'd been dismissed from Sir Edward's and was about to over-reach herself as a house-maid telling her employer how to run his marriage and risk him not being able to keep her on either.

Doors were closing all around her but Alice had never felt so secure as she did now. She could do this and she didn't have to do it alone. Daniel loved her.

★ ★ ★

The coachman slowed the horses as they entered the gates of the new park.

Alice pointed.

'The house she was in is over there if you wanted to see Mrs Younger before you tackle her brother.'

'What is it, a dower house?'

Alice shook her head. She had no idea what a dower house was but she thought it would be better if he stopped here first.

Suppose Sir Edward refused to see him? Most of the staff probably didn't know Mrs Younger was there and it could become very frustrating. If only the couple could speak first.

'All she wants is to know you love her.'

Maybe John Younger could just take his wife home and that would be an end to it.

Except she'd have to go with them.

'Wait here,' Mr Younger told the coachman. 'I'm going to walk across to the dower house.'

Alice hurried after him and after a few seconds' hesitation Frederic followed. It was the same man standing with his back against the door and he looked very startled when he saw the procession.

'I'm John Younger Esquire,' Mr Younger said, his voice calm and measured. 'I'm here to see my wife.' The man didn't respond.

'Would you stand aside and let me in, please,' Mr Younger added, reaching around the side of the man and pushing at the door. 'Eleanor!' he called when it didn't open.

Alice felt quite sorry for the guard. Behind him the door opened and there stood Mrs Fleming. She opened it wide for Mr Younger to go in. The poor man acting as guard began to run towards the house.

'You did it,' Mrs Fleming said, relief clear in her whole aspect.

'I lost my place here because of this,' Alice said. 'And the butler took your shilling.'

If she thought Mrs Fleming was going to be grateful and offer to remedy Alice's situation straight away, she was going to be disappointed. The housekeeper stood on the doorstep looking dazed.

Alice turned her back on the house-keeper and walked back towards the carriage, not sure whether she could count on any of them to help her. It wasn't even that they owed her something for what she'd done for them, it was their fault she was in the position she was in.

She smiled. She couldn't be angry. Whatever happened now she had them to thank them for what the change had done for her.

* * *

It wasn't long before Mr and Mrs Younger came out of the house. She was leaning on her husband and did look quite ill. He and Frederic helped her up into the coach.

'We'll go round to the front of the house,' Mr Younger said to the coachman. 'We should find food and water for the horses, if nothing else.'

Frederic helped Alice up into the seat beside the coachman and she laughed to think of the contrast with the way she'd left only the day before. She almost hoped Mr Sim would see her, but not quite, because her position still wasn't clear. He might still have the last laugh.

'It looks like Mrs Fleming's not coming,' Alice said. 'The housekeeper,' Alice explained to Frederic. 'She's been with Mrs Younger all this time.'

Frederic went up the steps to the grand entrance to the house and spoke to someone at the door. In a moment, a well dressed woman came out of the door and ran down to the carriage.

Sir Edward's wife? Alice struggled to recall her name. Lady Mathilda, she thought. The woman was greeting the Youngers as if she hadn't seen them for some time. So Sir Edward had not told his wife what he was doing?

It was only when the Youngers had been taken inside that Alice began to wonder what had happened to Mrs Fleming. As the coachman was instructed to take the horses to the stable, Alice thought she would go with Frederic to the back door and then think about looking for her. Frederic had had a long journey too. Someone should offer him refreshment.

Gillian was looking shocked, and paled when she saw Alice.

'Is Mr Sim around?' Alice asked. She didn't want to meet him.

'He's checking the wine cellar,' Gilliam said. 'Should I go and get him?'

'No, don't,' Alice said quickly. 'It's just I've brought Frederic in. He's Mr Younger's footman. He's had a long journey this morning.'

'Is it Mr Younger upstairs, then?'

'Mr and Mrs Younger. Shall I sit Frederic in the servants' dining-room?' Alice asked. 'I haven't got my apron on or I'd prepare some refreshment for him myself.'

'Oh, are you back working here?' One of the friendly maids hurried in. 'That's good. Look, Alice is back,' she told some others. 'I knew it would be a mistake.'

Alice laughed.

'It was a mistake but it's not resolved yet. I just showed Sir Edward's brother-in-law the way here and brought his footman in for dinner.'

Gillian looked anxiously at Alice as if to see how much more she would say.

Some of the maids were looking at Frederic with interest and she hoped it wouldn't embarrass him.

Alice kept out of the way of the chaos as the family's tea went up — Sir Edward and his visitor were out and about somewhere in the park, it seemed — and a light meal set out for the servants.

Gillian might have tried to exclude her

227

but the other maids made sure there was a place set for Alice and in the manoeuvring to be beside Frederic, Alice found Maggie was too far away up the table for proper conversation.

Once she'd finished her food, Alice caught Gillian's eye.

'I'm going to look for Mrs Fleming,' Alice whispered to Gillian and left quickly before anyone else asked where she was going.

The house was silent and Mrs Fleming didn't even answer when Alice spotted her in one of the upstairs rooms, where it looked as though she'd been packing Mrs Younger's things. For now, though, she was sitting on the edge of the bed.

'The mistress is having tea with her sister-in-law. Sir Edward is there. I don't think the housekeeper is here, either, but you should come over and have something to eat.'

It was disconcerting to see Mrs Fleming staring at nothing.

'I don't think this is a well run household. The housekeeper seems to delegate to a senior maid and even the butler gets involved with managing the female staff.'

Alice had been hoping for some reaction, not knowing whether Mrs Fleming was even listening, and at this she shot Alice a sharp look.

'I was surprised, too,' Alice went on. 'Mr Sim dismissed me when he saw I had the shilling you gave me. The housekeeper had made me promise never to mention your name or that of the mistress and the person in charge made me promise not to tell anyone where you were, so I couldn't defend myself.

'He stole it from us. There would have been change as well. I just need to repay the Hopkin family for paper and a stamp. I'd like to know what he did with your shilling.'

Mrs Fleming did not appear to be moved by the theft. It had been the extension of power by the butler that had struck her most.

'And who he thought gave him the authority to dismiss your employee.'

Mrs Fleming stood up.

'Indeed. We will go and speak to the housekeeper to ensure she knows he is overstepping the boundaries.'

Alice nodded.

Sir Edward's housekeeper was missing from her post again and the butler was in the cellar choosing wine for the evening meal.

'We'll wait in his room,' Mrs Fleming decided. She looked around the downstairs and her eyes lit on Frederic. 'Perhaps you could get a message to Mrs Younger that I'm here.'

'Frederic doesn't work here,' Alice put in.

'I can do it,' he said. 'Or speak to Mr Younger.' He glanced at Alice. 'I need to know where I stand, as well.'

Mrs Fleming nodded.

'Sit here beside me.' She motioned to one of the seats in front of the butler's table. 'It all seems most irregular here anyway. We may as well be as bad.'

Mrs Fleming was back in control.

After a few minutes Frederic looked in and entered.

'Mr Younger was most insistent a place be laid for you at the table upstairs.'

Mrs Fleming looked at her dress.

'I'm not dressed to dine.'

Frederic smiled.

'Mrs Younger said you would say that and Mr Younger said you were clothed in your loyalty and that was good enough.'

So his wife had convinced him Mrs Fleming was not a villain. This was going well.

Mr Sim appeared behind Frederic.

'Thank you, my man.'

Alice gave the kind footman a half smile. That was him dismissed.

'We're to stay the night here,' he said softly and Alice nodded, 'and leave in the morning.'

That was his situation clarified. Alice wondered if she was included in the 'we'.

As the thought occurred to her something in her stomach sank. How would she let Daniel know? Leave it to Maggie to tell him? No. That wasn't what she wanted.

Her stomach churned as Mr Sim

came into the room and stared at her for a moment. What was she doing thinking about what she wanted? She shouldn't even be here.

'You must be Mrs Fleming.' Mr Sim wasn't as haughty as he'd been before, but he ignored Alice. 'Mrs Younger is anxious to see you.'

'Hmm,' she said. 'And they leave in the morning.'

'And you as well.' Mr Sim coughed. 'They were most insistent,' he repeated.

Good. If Mrs Younger had convinced her husband the housekeeper had acted from devotion to her it meant they were speaking together properly again.

'Was Alice mentioned?'

Mr Sim's eyes swivelled towards Alice but he didn't answer. So her loyalty counted for nothing.

Mrs Fleming spoke.

'You dismissed Alice over a misunderstanding and took a coin I gave her.'

The butler sat back in his chair, looking embarrassed.

'Lady Mathilda's housekeeper has

been called away often of late over a family emergency.'

Beside her Alice could feel Mrs Fleming's eyebrows rise. It was hard not to laugh at her disapproval.

'Things below stairs have as a consequence become rather lax,' Mr Sim continued. 'I've done my best in the circumstances.'

'Your best has included doubting the honesty of a loyal maid and taking the shilling I gave her.'

Mr Sim stood up and went to a locked box. Alice felt Mrs Fleming bristle beside her.

'You know this isn't about the money, Mr Sim.'

'Nevertheless, I must repay it.'

'And Alice's good name?'

'Various persons spoke to me after the event and I saw I made a wrong judgement. It had been a difficult week.'

'It was a difficult week for Alice as well.'

Alice began to feel warm inside. Her work at the lodge had not gone unnoticed.

If Mr Sim could see her as a person and as trustworthy that was the last obstacle to her remaining here.

'Could I keep my place here then, Mr Sim?' she glanced at Mrs Fleming. 'I've made friends in the village where we stayed and would very much like to be close to them.'

Mr Sim nodded.

'I don't see why not. I'll speak to the housekeeper.' He coughed. 'I see no reason why you should not start back at work here formally tomorrow.'

'Thank you, Mr Sim. But I'll start on Monday.' There was someone very important to see the next day. 'I have Sundays off.'

Daniel And Ivy After All?

It would have been good for Sir Edward's household if Mrs Fleming had stayed, too, but Alice was under no illusions she would remain friends with the housekeeper after today. There was no tearful farewell and hope of seeing one another again. She made sure Alice had her back pay, which was only fair, but neither Mr nor Mrs Younger sought her out to thank her for bringing them back together.

'Is the mistress all right?' Alice asked as she took her wages on the Saturday night.

'She seems very happy,' Mrs Fleming said. 'And he's being very attentive.'

It was all Alice was going to get. There was no bonus for work beyond the call of duty — she hadn't expected it — but Mrs Fleming handed Alice the disputed shilling.

'You still owe some of this to your friends,' she said.

Alice sought Frederic out the next morning to say goodbye.

'Would you be able to take greetings from me to Betty?' she asked. 'She's the one I'll be sorry not to see.'

'With pleasure.' The young man's cheeks were a little pink as he said it. That would be good, if he and Betty . . .

'Tell her I'm learning to read and I'll write to her.'

'She'll like that.'

The person who was furthest from Alice's thoughts as she approached the village was the one she saw first. It was surely too early for Ivy to be on her way to the morning church service. The girl hurried to join Alice as soon as she saw her.

'Alice. I just wanted to say thank you for giving me Daniel back.' Alice stopped walking, feeling as if the blood was draining from her head, her face.

'And for helping me see how wrong I was. I knew it when I saw you with Daniel and then when he spoke to me I

236

saw how it should be.'

'What do you mean?' If this was how it was going to end Alice wished with all her heart she had been squeezed into the carriage with Mr and Mrs Younger that morning.

'I'd started to think of that man as my 'sweetheart'. I was waiting for him when I saw Daniel kiss you. It made me see how far I'd travelled in the wrong direction.'

'I don't understand.'

'That man never cared for me and when Daniel said you called his voice ugly I saw that he was ugly and so was what he was asking me to do.'

'So you didn't go ahead with the robbery?'

'No, nor ever will. He's going back to prison anyway. He was so angry when I told him, he tried to set fire to our house but the neighbours caught him and stopped him.'

'And your father?'

'He has found work as a labourer on Sir Edward's estate.'

237

'That's good.'

'That's another thing that man wanted to get revenge for — Pa not wanting to work with him any more. It's all changed so quickly Alice, and all because of you.'

'I'm pleased for you, Ivy.'

'And you? I saw your employer's carriage go past earlier and wondered if you were inside again.'

Alice shook her head.

'No. That only happens once in a lifetime.'

'They're leaving you to make your own way?'

'I'm not going with them. I'm working at Sir Edward's house.'

'Oh, that's good.'

Ivy seemed genuinely pleased. It would be hard for them to be friends if she was with Daniel but Alice mentally listed the remaining advantages of working there. Being close to Miss Little and learning to read, for one. And building a new life where no-one knew what she had been before. A mouse, asleep to her own abilities and potential.

How easy would it be to build such a life if she had to see the man she loved with Ivy?

At least Ivy had changed for the better and would not harm Daniel.

As if thinking about him made him appear, she saw his dear figure hurrying towards them and a strength rose in her.

Was she going back to allowing others to decide her future or would she fight for what she wanted? She'd fought for the job she wanted and could cope with a more important battle. This wasn't going to be left unfinished, the truth of her love hidden away again.

'What did you mean, I gave you Daniel back?'

'We were such good friends when we were children and I messed it all up,' Ivy said. 'I was unkind and proud and stupid.

'Now because of you we can all be friends again, me and Daniel and Stanley, and you as well. I'll leave you to talk to him.' She walked ahead, leaving Alice standing, and passed Daniel with only a brief greeting.

Violet was right, and Mrs Hopkin. You had to talk openly with people about things.

Alice's breath started to come easily again and she started to run. She met Daniel in the middle of the road and ran to him, arms opened wide. He broke into a broad smile as he picked her up and swung her round.

'I was coming to look for you,' he said as he put her down.

'I was coming back to you.'

Alice felt as though the emotion would burst out of her. With a small sigh she reached up to kiss Daniel and his lips met hers willingly. Her arms went around him and Alice felt that her legs had gone so weak she would sink to the ground if he didn't continue to hold her tight.

When they were breathless from kissing they broke apart and gazed at one another. Alice saw the wonder she was feeling reflected in Daniel's beloved face and in his clear eyes.

The sound of a carriage disturbed them and they broke apart but Daniel kept his arm around Alice. She leaned into him, careless of who was coming.

The carriage stopped outside Miss Little's house and Miss Little got out, followed by a woman who must be her younger sister, slim and upright, but walking with difficulty. The coachman lent an arm to her and she limped up the front path.

'Alice, Daniel, I'm very pleased to see you together.' Miss Little beamed. So she had seen what Alice had thought she was keeping from her.

'My sister is coming to live with me,' the kind woman went on. 'But there will always be time for you to visit. Or are you going back to Mr Younger's house?'

'I'm working at Sir Edward's now.'

'That is much more convenient. Now, my sister used to teach at a Sunday school. She has some books to give you, if you have time to look in later.'

'Thank you.'

'My sister is also looking to open a hosier and draper's shop nearby. She will need someone to help who knows her letters.'

'I want to learn my letters whatever else happens,' Alice said.

Miss Little nodded.

'It's you who makes it happen.' She followed her sister into the house.

'Can we go to the lodge and see my robins?' Alice asked Daniel.

They stopped for another kiss at the side of the lodge.

'It looks as though they've left,' Alice said, examining the place where the nest had been.

'You're not too disappointed?'

She shook her head.

'I'm proud of them. It must take courage to fly.'

Daniel took Alice's hand.

'You should know, you learned,' he said tenderly. 'It's what Miss Little said. You dream it and you make it happen.'

She squeezed his hand.

'Once you're properly awake, it's easy,' she said.

We do hope that you have enjoyed reading this large print book.

Did you know that all of our titles are available for purchase?

We publish a wide range of high quality large print books including:
Romances, Mysteries, Classics
General Fiction
Non Fiction and Westerns

Special interest titles available in large print are:
The Little Oxford Dictionary
Music Book, Song Book
Hymn Book, Service Book

Also available from us courtesy of Oxford University Press:
Young Readers' Dictionary
(large print edition)
Young Readers' Thesaurus
(large print edition)

For further information or a free brochure, please contact us at:
Ulverscroft Large Print Books Ltd.,
The Green, Bradgate Road, Anstey,
Leicester, LE7 7FU, England.
Tel: (00 44) **0116 236 4325**
Fax: (00 44) **0116 234 0205**

Other titles in the
Linford Romance Library:

TURPIN'S APPRENTICE

Sarah Swatridge

England, 1761. Charity Bell is the daughter of an inn keeper. Her two elder sisters are only interested in marrying well, whereas feisty Charity is determined to discover who the culprit is behind the most recent highwayman ambush. And by catching the highwayman, she aims to persuade Sir John to bring his family, and his wealth, to her village. It may also make the handsome Moses notice her!

REVENGE OF THE SPANISH PRINCESS

Linda Tyler

Cornwall, 1695. When her beloved father dies with the name Lovett on his lips, privateer captain Catherina Trelawny vows revenge on the mysterious pirate. Seeking him on the Mediterranean island of Azul, she is charmed by the personable Henry Darley. But Cate finds her plan goes awry when Darley and Lovett turn out to be the same man. Cate and Henry set sail across the high seas battling terrifying storms, deadly shipwreck, dissolute corsairs — and each other.

THE NURSE AND THE CAPTAIN

Philippa Carey

It is 1918 and the Great War is ending. The evening before the last great battle, Ben hears that the flu epidemic has killed his entire family. Devastated, he is reckless in battle. Badly wounded, he is sent to an auxiliary hospital in England.

Laura's grandfather, the earl, has died, and she doesn't know what to do now. She volunteers at the local wartime hospital and is put in charge of a very sick officer . . .

LOVE IN LAVENDER LANE

Jill Barry

Fiona exchanges her quiet suburban world for 1970s London when she inherits her great-aunt's marriage bureau near Marble Arch. But she has never been truly in love, so it's going to be a challenge arranging perfect pairings for her starry-eyed clients . . . While Fiona's busy interviewing and arranging introductions, how will she ever find time to make her own dream come true? And could it be that she and her most difficult client to match are actually meant for one another?

THE LOVE TREE

Patricia Keyson

When Lily arrives at The Limes to work as a maid for two sisters, Eta and Mabel, little does she know she will instantly fall in love with their handsome lodger, Samuel. When Cecil Potts visits the sisters' beer house and shop, a tale of murder, death and deceit unravels. Will Lily and Samuel ever step out from Cecil's dark shadow to find happiness under the love tree?